T0193674

BORN OF THE WAR

A STORY ABOUT THE HORRORS OF WAR, A PASSIONATE AFFAIR AND A MOTHER'S LOVE

KENNY RAGLAND, USNR RETIRED

BORN OF THE WAR
A STORY ABOUT THE HORRORS OF WAR, A PASSIONATE AFFAIR AND A MOTHER'S LOVE

iUniverse books may be ordered through booksellers or by contacting:

iUniverse
1663 Liberty Drive
Bloomington, IN 47403
www.iuniverse.com
1-800-Authors (1-800-288-4677)

Because of the dynamic nature of the Internet, any web addresses or links contained in this book may have changed since publication and may no longer be valid. The views expressed in this work are solely those of the author and do not necessarily reflect the views of the publisher, and the publisher hereby disclaims any responsibility for them.

Any people depicted in stock imagery provided by Thinkstock are models, and such images are being used for illustrative purposes only. Certain stock imagery © Thinkstock.

ISBN: 978-1-5320-1934-0 (sc)
ISBN: 978-1-5320-1935-7 (e)

Library of Congress Control Number: 2017908053

Print information available on the last page.

iUniverse rev. date: 06/14/2017

Special thanks to

- John & Darci and Brooks for posing for my book cover, to Angela for extensive editing and story expansion ideas, and to my wife Joyce for all her financial and emotional support.
- My East Coast Navy shipmates, who were large or partial character inspirations for many of the central and secondary figures in my book.
- To southeast Kansas family, who were certainly character inspirations for principal figures portrayed.
- To my own children, who were strong inspirations for the grown siblings written about.
- To the pentagon book review personnel, who worked with me on security clearance and general Navy consideration topics.
- My high school Creative Writing teacher Mr. Redford. You said you never had a student who went on to become a book writer, but that you had several who could be close. If you are still living, I hope you can see what I worked so very hard on.

PREFACE

I began work on this book in July 2007. I had just deployed with Naval Mobile Construction Battalion 15 and was doing my premobilization at the Seabee Base in Gulfport, Mississippi.

Each of the characters in this book is built from combined personalities of people I actually knew. The real-life people will see things that will remind them of themselves. But the characters are all handsomer and braver than the actual people really were.

In life, I was never involved in any romance on any of my four deployments. I got to see some, but almost all sailors and military personnel were very professional and good moral examples.

Never did I personally participate in combat or IED situations. One indirect fire grenade exploded very near me at Camp Nathan Smith on my fourth deployment in Afghanistan.

The battles in the book are similar to actual ones that occurred, though not to my command.

The use of Humvees described was more from 2006 and prior years of the Iraqi conflict. I rode in the newer mine-resistant, ambush-protected MRAP vehicles, which were much safer to convoy in.

I covered the construction of actual combat outposts, just like those described in the pages of this book. Convoy travel threats from IEDs were very real. Had we been in Humvees like previous commands, the IEDs our convoys hit would have created casualties similar to those I wrote about.

I have described naval reserve centers exactly as they were.

But if I may say, the twenty-year retirement I very much earned and received happened because some of the reserve center staff, as well as some of the regional- and Pentagon-level naval administration, went to bat for me and other sailors. They made sure I had the proper number of required annual points for the two-week trainings I performed every year.

I completed my naval career with twenty-three years of service, before high year tenure requirements forced my separation.

My thanks goes out to all the people who make up the characters I write about, to family, and to iUniverse for publishing the manuscript I've worked so very hard on.

I hope you like the story.

PROLOGUE

Al Asad, Iraq, January 20, 2007

I t was still dark in the barren Iraqi desert as the navy Seabee convoy headed out. The light tan Humvees looked ominous in the shadowy nighttime light.

The Seabees were making an early-morning supply-and-personnel convoy out to a forward operating base (FOB) they were constructing for the marines. A naval public affairs photojournalist was going with them to do a story on the new security installation.

There were six military vehicles total. The first and last Humvees in the column were equipped with crew-served weapons, M240 Bravo machine guns. The trucks carrying water, construction materials, and meals ready to eat (MREs) came fourth and fifth.

The second vehicle carried the Seabee welders, and the third vehicle had the convoy master chief (the team leader) and the writer-photographer.

All the Seabees in the convoy were afraid and well aware of the danger. Many improvised explosive devices, also known as IEDs, had taken countless lives over the past year, including lives of their shipmates.

But no one hesitated to board their Humvees. They bravely and resolutely accepted their duty, and they all refused to have any other Seabee take their place.

The steady moving convoy drove through the large air base, out of the heavily built main gate, and onto the route preselected because it had the least amount of insurgent activity, a yellow route for caution. The road was named Plutonium.

They had early light to see by when they approached the turn onto Red-Path, a much more dangerous blacktop road marked red for the likelihood of insurgent IED activity. The lead vehicle was responsible for identifying possible IEDs spotted along the forbidding roadways ahead.

Diligent Seabees watched closely through the windows of their Humvees and supply trucks. The convoy team members nervously but stoically approached a small creek channel just before the turn onto Red-Path.

As the third vehicle crossed over the culvert, the roadway erupted into a massive fireball explosion, hurling the rear of the Humvee high into the air. The following truck was unable to stop before its front wheels slid over into the large steep crater.

The sound of small arms rifle fire broke out, and the glare of reddish-orange muzzle flashes shined brightly in the breaking light of dawn. Cowardly insurgents were shooting at the survivors struggling for life in the downed vehicles.

The booming navy crew-served machine guns quickly opened up from their designated fields of fire. They returned overwhelming and lethal force toward the insurgents firing from both sides of the road. It was all over in less than thirty seconds.

The third Humvee lay on its side burning. The driver had been shot as he tried to escape the flames. The driver and A-driver (passenger and radio communicator) in the following Humvee had been shot when they both ignored protocol and tried to escape the bullets flying toward and into their stranded Humvee.

The second-in-command leading petty officer of the group shook all over as he pronounced it safe for the convoy personnel to rescue the downed victims. Frantic Seabees in the remaining vehicles unloaded and rushed with first aid supplies toward the burning wreck, with the LPO leading the way.

They found a horrible sight.

"They're all dead," exclaimed the young LPO as he looked at

the darkly burned body of his longtime command master chief, who was visible through the windshield.

The shocked Seabees used anything they could find to protect their hands and arms from the heat of the still-burning Humvee. They hooked on and righted the vehicle with a truck and chain. Then they pried open doors to pull out the blackened bodies of the master chief, naval photographer, and A-driver. Additional Seabees recovered the bullet-riddled bodies of the fourth Humvee team, who lay where they had fallen by the open doors of their stranded vehicle.

CHAPTER 1

Columbus, Kansas, July 2006

The workweek went by quickly for Kelly Raines, a forty-four-year-old photojournalist from rural southeast Kansas. He was a field writer for *Agriculture Today Magazine* and a navy reservist. He always tried to be off the road and back at his house by noon on Fridays so he could finish writing the final draft and get his story in on time.

Kelly looked for the attachment icon on his e-mail. Just to get the pictures, he'd had to drive over three counties to find farmers still running milking operations.

He double-checked that the pictures had the cutlines embedded in the files. *Yes, they are*, Kelly thought to himself. *I hope they like this story after all of the miles it took to get it.*

Kelly had a good relationship with his editor at *Ag-Today*. He had been there for a year now. She was the one, Sharon Willard, who had first talked to the broad-shouldered, hazel-eyed job applicant about filling a traveling writer position. She had liked the fact he had degrees in agriculture and journalism and a military background.

He had just come off a six-month active duty for special work, ADSW naval activation from the USS *Georgia* submarine. A new job was very appealing. He had spent ten years in public affairs with the rural electric cooperatives when the sub opportunity came along, and he had jumped on it. Writing for a farm magazine had sounded just as good.

Kelly had just pushed send on his e-mail when his cell phone rang. *It's going through right now,* thought Kelly as he fumbled for the blaring phone in his pocket.

"This is Kelly," he said.

There was a pause on the other end. Kelly thought that was odd. Sharon always starting talking a mile a minute as soon as he said hello.

"Is this Petty Officer Raines?" said the voice.

Now it was Kelly's turn to pause as he wondered what the reserve center wanted. He had turned in his travel claim for his annual training almost a month ago. They hadn't paid it yet, as usual.

"Yes, this is MC1 Raines," said Kelly. This was navy speak for a mass communications specialist, petty officer first class. He and other MCs had always hated that the navy had combined the journalist rate with photographer's mate and lithographer. Writers had been called JOs or journalists forever.

"This is YN1 Zumwalt. You're being mobilized to active duty," said the reserve center staff member. YN1 stood for yeoman first class, a navy administrator. "I need to go over some things with you. Do you have something to write with?"

Like most reservists, Kelly knew a full mobilization to active duty in the war would likely come one day. But still, *You're never quite ready for it when it does,* he thought.

He fumbled for his notepad and pen. He was used to people from the navy calling occasionally. But this time his stomach began to churn as he prepared to write.

"I'm ready," he said and then waited to see what the yeoman was going to startle him with next.

"You need to report within forty-eight hours with all of your uniforms and gear," said Zumwalt. "You will need a copy of your will, a second pair of glasses—are you writing all of this down?" Zumwalt asked.

"Yes, I'm writing as you speak," said Kelly.

"You will also need a copy of your last DD-214, certified marriage license, birth certificate for your wife …" The yeoman went on with his list of things for mobilized sailors to bring with them. "Do you have any questions?"

"Yes," said Kelly. "Have you mobilized the whole unit or just me? And where are we going, if I can ask?"

"The navy has mobilized most of your unit," said Zumwalt. "You'll be going to a command in western Iraq."

Kelly processed the words he'd heard. He was an active duty sailor again, ready or not, and headed to the war.

"I'll let my employer and family know and get to packing my seabag."

"Well, all right then. We'll see you here on Monday morning at 0730," Zumwalt said and then hung up.

It was late afternoon when Kelly had gotten the call. That gave him the weekend to pack and spend time with family. Four o'clock in the afternoon on Friday until Monday morning was a little longer than forty-eight hours, and he was glad for it.

The first person he called was his wife of three years, Gwendolyn. Olive skinned with dark brunette hair, the forty-six-year-old farm girl was an orthodontic assistant for a prominent orthodontist in Joplin, Missouri. He deliberated whether or not he should call her at work, but since no one was dead, just deployed, he thought she could take the news.

The phone rang three times before the receptionist picked up the receiver. The office was having a typical busy Friday afternoon.

"Dr. Clark's office," said the soprano-voiced new girl, Brandi.

"Hi, Brandi, this is Kelly. Can I talk to Gwen if she's not with a patient?"

"Let me check. Yes, she's putting up instruments. Put you on hold for a second."

"Hello," said Gwen in her end-of-the-day voice just a few moments later.

"Hi, babe. I have some big news," said Kelly, pausing a bit before he spoke. "The navy just mobilized me. You're going to be a sailor's wife for a while."

The silence was deafening. He knew her blue eyes had just

opened wide as her tired brain figured out what had happened. Finally Gwen spoke.

"Did you get called up?" his obviously concerned wife asked.

"Yep, I sure did. Just got off the phone. Haven't even called work yet."

"Are you going to Iraq?"

Iraq and Afghanistan were the nemeses of reservist wives, as they all hoped their husbands wouldn't have to go there.

"Yes," said Kelly, "me and most of the unit."

"When do you leave?"

"They gave me the long forty-eight hours," said Kelly. "I report Monday morning."

"How long will you be gone?"

"It will be for a year, according to our last brief on possible call-ups. I'll know more when you get home."

"Have you told the kids yet?"

"Nope, just you. I'll be a lot further along on the called-people list when you get off work."

Gwen let out a long sigh. "Well, finish your calls then."

She started to say something else but didn't finish it, and Kelly didn't want to follow up.

"I'll see you when I get to the house," Gwen said.

"Everything will be fine, Gwen," Kelly said. "I love you."

"I love you too, Kelly."

Kelly didn't think long before thoughts about the church fence he had just finished crossed his mind. It had been just this past Saturday when he had finished the several-weekend project.

An adjacent lot had been given to the congregation in 1910 and had never been taken care of properly. Kelly had cut the brush away from the corners and out of the old barbed and hog-wire fence. He had attached treated wooden posts and white painted board rails to change the ugly former lot into a very attractive parking location for church gatherings.

He had struggled to come up with the proper Bible verse to write on the board railings, looking at John 3:16, Corinthians 13:13, and John 15:13.

I'm so glad I didn't leave that half-done, thought Kelly. *Maybe God was just in it.*

He thought he should probably call his kids next.

Kelly had two grown children from his first marriage. Gwen had two also. All four were grown and either in college or working. He started with his oldest and worked his way down.

Joshua was a twenty-one-year-old newly hired fireman in Kansas City. Kelly dialed the cell number from his speed dial settings.

"Hello," said the broad-shouldered fireman, who looked just like his dad.

"Josh, got some news. Navy called me up," said Kelly.

Josh didn't pause for very long after he heard his dad say the important words. "Are you going to the front lines in Baghdad?" he asked.

"Nope. I'll be in the Western Command Headquarters," said Kelly. He knew full well he would be subject to the same IEDs that killed most troops. But he didn't tell his son that.

Kelly went on to answer all of Josh's questions and called or left messages for all of the other kids as well. He really appreciated the support of Gwen's children; they both wished him the best. They were certainly a contrast to some of his past girlfriends' kids, with whom he had clashed, back in "*before Gwen*" time.

Next he called his stepmother and aunt. His folks were both gone now, but his dad's second wife and one last surviving aunt were both still going strong. They wished him well and told him to be safe on his deployment.

After family was out of the way, Kelly thought he would call one of his shipmates. Leigh Andrews was his best friend in the navy. Even though she was a woman, they had always been close.

"Hey, Kelly."

"Hi, Leigh. I guess you're going too?"

"Sure am. When did they call you?"

"About four o'clock this afternoon. I'm glad I had my story all done."

"They told me late this morning," said Leigh. "I almost called you then, but I didn't think I should be the one to break the news."

"I was going one hundred miles an hour on my story," said Kelly. "It's better that I got it done and sent before I found out."

Kelly knew full well that if he had heard Leigh was getting called up and he hadn't immediately phoned her, she would be ticked as could be. But he didn't say that.

"Do you know who else is coming?" asked Leigh.

"I know Senior Chief, Skipper, both new chiefs, the lieutenants, and also Commander Quinn. On the petty officer side, it's everybody."

Leigh had been selected for an officer commissioning as an ensign. Her package had recently been accepted. She was waiting to be pinned, giving her a direct commission from an MC1, the rank Kelly still held. He and other sailors had encouraged her to submit an application.

Leigh was a very accomplished television personality in Columbus, Ohio. She and Kelly lived in towns with the same name but in different states. There was even a Columbus, Georgia. Every year the queen from each community got together at one of the three towns for Columbus Days.

Unlike Kelly, Leigh had grown up in a single-parent family. She'd been raised by her mom and grandmother. Her father had been a teenage boy, shunned by her family.

She had always wanted to see him, but her family prevented him from contacting his daughter. Leigh hadn't seen him, her stepsiblings, or her paternal grandparents until she was older and then only from a distance.

Besides being a morning news show host, Leigh was an excellent writer and photographer. Kelly had always felt that she was capable of doing more than her TV station allowed her. But she liked the morning show, and there was no talking her into applying for anchor openings at prime-time slots, or at other stations. Her husband, Bill, had tried to get her to do that too. The officer's commission was the only thing he or anyone had succeeded in getting her to try for.

"Are you ready for this?" asked Leigh.

"Oh, I guess so," said Kelly. "I wasn't looking to volunteer, but I thought we would be going sooner or later. I guess we can get our rotation out of the way now."

"I thought that too," said Leigh. "Gossip I've heard is that we wouldn't go again for four to six years."

"I hope that's right," said Kelly. "We need to have a civilian life too. Don't know when I'm flying out, but I'm pretty sure it will be Monday afternoon."

"They wouldn't tell me when my flight was either, just that it's probably on Monday. I don't think they know."

"Obviously my reserve center is no better than yours," said Kelly.

"Meet you in Norfolk, Kelly. Tell Gwen I said hi."

"Same for Bill."

Both sailors hung up their phones.

Kelly turned around from his desk and looked in his closet for his seabags. *Why do they want all of my uniforms?* he wondered. *They're going to issue us desert camouflage.* He decided to pack his whites and blues in one bag in case he was told to send them back home.

Gwen pulled her Impala out of the office parking lot. The trip home usually took about thirty minutes. She hadn't been married to this new man all that long. They were starting their third year. Unlike her first marriage, time went so much faster for this second one.

She had been divorced for going on fifteen years when he came along. Gwen was almost two years older than Kelly. Like him, she hadn't really thought she would ever marry again.

Three years earlier, Gwen had to undergo a hysterectomy for uterine tumors. The biopsies all turned out benign. With childbearing out of the way, Gwen had felt she would live the rest of her life single.

She hadn't been looking at all when he walked into her life. She remembered very well the tall, athletic man with a dark tan coming into the office to ask if they were accepting patients.

"Who is that?" she had asked her coworkers when she first saw him. "Is he single?"

With her fellow partners in crime, she had arranged to be the one to take his records when he came in for his first appointment. There she was, not looking for any man at all, but swooning over this one like a high school girl going after a ball player.

At first she had thought he was still married. Kelly had talked about his wife and kids back in Sedalia in western Missouri. But the office manager had settled that question from Kelly's financial records when he set up his insurance coverage.

"He's divorced and single," Naomi had said when the girls all asked her about his marital status.

Gwen was from a large Protestant family in southeast Kansas. Her dad had farmed, and her mom had worked part-time for an accountant in Columbus. She was the youngest of her family, and both parents had passed away before she met Kelly.

Kelly had grown up in the Kansas City area. His dad had been a building manager, and his mom was a stay-at-home housewife. His mom died in her early fifties, and his dad only met Gwen once. He passed away shortly after their marriage, too sick with cancer to attend.

Kelly and Gwen had a beautiful Christmas wedding. Gwen couldn't have been happier. The financial help from two incomes had been such a blessing to the farm and utility bills. Gwen knew how hard she had struggled just to keep her head above water.

Gwen's thoughts turned to Kelly's pending absence. She liked having a man again, and a husband.

He will be gone a year, she thought. *This is the last thing I would ever want him to do. Yes, his income would be there, but he wouldn't.*

Her thoughts turned to her trying to do the mowing, brush burning, and repairs again. Keeping her car running had always been difficult. Kelly was a whiz at mechanics.

Kelly can fix anything, she thought. *I can't fix nothin'!*

She liked having a man again. Someone to touch and hold her.

I don't want him to go to Iraq, thought the still-shocked Kansas farm girl.

They had talked about this. She had seen *US Navy* written in his calendar on their first date.

Gwen turned her car down the new gravel driveway Kelly had finished putting down that winter. He had hauled umpteen loads of stone with his trailer and shoveled it all by hand.

She looked at the farm and home her still-new husband had worked so hard on. The house was painted a semigloss white, and the front shutters were country blue. Kelly had cut down all the tree and weed sprouts from around the house and outbuildings. He had leveled out dirt piles and filled in holes. With the yard all freshly mowed, it looked so much better than before when she was single.

She looked out across the farm she had lived on all her life and at the fields she had played in as a young girl. She and her sisters used to hide in the soybean rows when cars drove by.

Kelly had planted no-till corn in her pasture. It looked good too, better than she had thought it would. Gwen hadn't been all that in favor of changing her pasture to row crops. She had wanted to get a horse again. But the fence would have needed a lot of work and dollars they didn't have.

She opened her car door and walked up the brick walkway Kelly had laid from the driveway to the front porch.

"Hey, babe," she hollered as she closed both doors quickly to keep in the air-conditioning.

"I'm back here," said Kelly from the office.

Kelly had remodeled Gwen's son, John's, old bedroom into an office. Johnny had been living at home when Kelly came on the scene. But John had soon moved in with his sister, Laura. Together with Laura's fiancé, Ben, the grown kids had bought a house and lived nearby in Galena, Kansas.

"Well, sailor boy, what do you think now about being a military reserve?" said Gwen as she looked hard at her already packing husband.

Kelly didn't say anything at first as he looked up from the dungarees he was rolling up. He shoved the dark blue pants into his seabag, walked over to Gwen, and gave her a big hug.

Gwen was a heavyset girl. She had struggled with her weight

all her life. He was a big man, though, and his arms still went way around her. She reached hers, still clad in her short-sleeved nursing scrubs, around him and hugged him back.

They paused in the embrace for a while until Kelly finally kissed her. "I don't know what to say," said Kelly. "So I guess I'll just get ready and go."

"You going to take your bicycle again?" asked Gwen as she remembered his navy trips over the past few years.

"Yep," said Kelly. "I'll be walkin' if I don't."

Kelly knew how to dismantle his bike, pack the frame into a long seabag, and stow the wheels in a rectangular military flight bag. He had done it for years for his annual navy trainings. It was a great way to get around the large bases and nearby communities when a car wasn't available.

Before either had a chance to say anything else, the phone rang. Gwen knew this would happen all weekend. She knew it wasn't for her and motioned for him to get the call.

"Hi, punkin'," said Kelly.

Gwen knew it was his daughter, Jeanne. She had heard Kelly call Jeanne is little girl and punkin' many times now. She was attending a community college and living with Kelly's first wife, Pat. Jeanne was in her second year studying liberal arts. She wasn't sure what she wanted to major in yet.

Gwen knew Jeanne would want to see Kelly before he left, and he would want to see his now grown little girl.

She overheard Kelly suggest the kids come there for a cookout.

Gwen didn't mind hosting the kids. Hers and his weren't together all that much. This would be a good reason to help that relationship along.

CHAPTER 2

Saturday morning dawned like any other Saturday. Kelly had slept well, almost as if he weren't going to war at all. If Gwen had tossed a bit, she hadn't bothered him. The phone had rung all evening as different family members and friends called. Gwen had tried to talk to some of them when she saw Kelly was worn out from it.

Kelly didn't know how he had packed as much as he had with so many interruptions, but there was one flight bag full of bicycle wheels and pressed uniforms. Next to it were two seabags. The bike frame noticeably poked along the side of one. He had accumulated many navy duffel bags through the years, and he was glad he did. He didn't know how he had ever made it with just one.

Gwen had already started breakfast when he headed for the shower. She knew he liked to eat a big breakfast. She already had sausage frying.

"Smells good in here," said Kelly as he stepped through the kitchen. "How did you sleep?"

"I woke up several times in the night," admitted Gwen. "Go wash up and I'll be ready to eat when you get out."

Kelly and Gwen spent the entire day together. They got all of his paperwork, wills, and marriage license copies. They even had time to pick up the house and go to the store. He had needed a few things to pack for his trip. They also bought groceries for the kids, who had all said they would come by on Sunday.

Saturday night came all too quickly, and they went to bed early.

This time they both tossed and turned. At about two thirty in the morning, Kelly started to get up to go read in the living room. Gwen reached her arms around him and pulled him back.

"Not yet, sailor boy. This is your next to last night here."

Kelly snuggled back in next to her.

Sunday morning they were both up early. Kelly had thought of a few things to add to his seabags through the night, and he packed them in. He had bought desert-colored washcloths to use for face clothes. On the farm he used those when he worked outside in the hot sweaty weather. He had forgotten to pack shoe polish, but he would probably be told to send his black shoes and boots back home.

The preacher at the rural church they attended was Gwen's brother-in-law. David had been a Christian church minister for going on twenty years now. His wife, Jane, Gwen's sister, had picked out the songs for the service with a military theme in mind. The first one was "Onward Christian Soldiers."

Kelly had joined the church before he and Gwen had even married. He liked the congregation's beliefs. While he had grown up a Southern Baptist, he hadn't liked the split between the Baptist conservatives and moderates.

Clergy politics were much less of a problem in the Christian Church.

Everyone told him how nice the fence, painted Bible verse, and spiffed-up parking lot looked. They wished him well and told him to come home safe. Gwen drove home after everyone had shook Kelly's hand.

"You have a lot of support," said Gwen.

"Yes, I do," said Kelly. "It's good to belong to a congregation like this."

The church he came from in Sedalia hadn't been as supportive of Kelly. They had all been nice enough through his divorce. He had always been encouraged to come to services. But it was just like the Baptist minister had said in the counseling sessions: "There will be a pressure on one or the other of the divorcing spouses to leave." In this case it was Kelly.

Strange, he had thought, how in the Catholic faith, in order to get the girl, you married the church. In the Baptist faith, if the wife decided to divorce you, then the congregation divorced you too.

Kelly changed clothes while Gwen fixed lunch. He backed her car up to load his seabags. Gwen's trunk was always full of rummage sale stuff for her booth at the local flea market. He moved some of it to the shed to make room for two seabags. He put the third in the backseat.

Kelly came into the house and sat down at the table. Gwen was eating a few of the celery sticks she was cutting. The kids would be there at two in the afternoon, so they were combining lunch and supper for the barbecue that afternoon.

Kelly tried to think of what else he should take, and he was glad he didn't have to lay out his uniform. Sailors were told to travel in civvies now, because of force protection policies to blend in with the local populations wherever they were.

"You're going to think of things you've forgotten all day," said Gwen. "You might as well just leave the trunk lid up."

"I'm sure I will," said Kelly. "But there is nothing worse than forgetting something."

Kelly had just lit the BBQ grill when he heard a car pull into the driveway. He had already swept off the deck and picnic table.

"Hey, old man," hollered Josh as he closed his pickup door. Josh walked up with his latest girlfriend, Jeni, or "Jen," as she went by. He had gone through more girls. Kelly had liked all of them and hoped this one would be around for a while.

It wasn't long before all four kids showed up. The driveway was full as sports cars, SUVs, and pickups filled the space. Gwen just beamed to have them all there at one time.

The kids didn't beam at seeing each other like their mom and stepmom did. The saying that combined families don't blend, they collide, was true for Kelly and Gwen's kids too.

Josh tried to break the ice first and spoke to Gwen's daughter, Laura. He and Jen had some big news they thought they should get out, before Kelly shoved off for Iraq.

"How's life in the four-states?" Josh asked.

"It's good," replied Laura. "We've been enjoying our new house in Galena."

Laura and her long-time boyfriend Ben had bought a nice four-bedroom, two-car garage home at a really good buy. It was a way John could live with them better too.

John was sitting by himself and not talking to anyone, as usual.

"Do you like the new house too, John?" asked Kelly's daughter, Jeanne.

John looked up, not really happy to be brought into the conversation.

"It's all right," he said.

It was no secret that John would have preferred to stay living with his mom had Kelly not come along.

"It's close to my several of my fishing ponds," John said, actually smiling this time.

Following the midafternoon meal, everyone was still sitting at the table when Josh thought they should probably say what they needed to get out.

"Pop," Josh said, "we've got some big news."

Kelly and Gwen grinned as they looked up, expecting to hear a wedding announcement. What came next floored everyone there.

"We're pregnant," said Josh. "Jen is two months along."

Kelly got ahold of himself first and looked approvingly at his son and Jen.

"Well, I look forward to my grandbaby," he said. "I may not be here for the birth, but you have to send me pictures." He walked over and gave the biggest of hugs to his son and daughter-in-law to be.

Jeanne, Gwen, and Laura followed.

"Son, are you going to include marriage plans in there sometime?" Kelly asked.

"We are," answered Jen for him. "We aren't sure just when yet, but soon."

Everyone knew Kelly wouldn't be able to make it.

"I can be there," said Gwen, "and I will see to it that we have lots of pictures to send."

Laura and Ben looked at each other with a "what do we do now" look. They had been together for several years, and marriage plans had never been more than talked about.

Gwen looked at Laura too but was determined not to say one word about marriage.

As the time waned, Laura said maybe they had better call it a day. Kelly had dreaded this, but he knew it was all part of being a sailor. Handshakes disappeared and hugs took their place. All the boys hugged their dad and stepdad. Typically, Gwen was the first one to tear up.

"Good luck over there, Kelly," said Laura as she gave her stepdad a big hug and kiss on the cheek. "I love you," she said.

That's when Kelly lost it. Laura was the first of Gwen's kids to say those words. She had grown close to Kelly, despite John's reluctance.

"I love you too, Dad," said Jeanne as she hugged Kelly's neck hard, tears streaming down both cheeks.

Josh didn't cry, but Jen did for them.

"Let me know when you pick out grandson names," Kelly said to his son and Jen.

"We will," said Josh as he and Jen both hugged Kelly at the same time.

When the last vehicle pulled out of the driveway, Kelly and Gwen just stood on their porch for a while. It was always good to have family come to their home, something Kelly had missed with his first family and paternal siblings.

When they went to bed that night, Gwen held Kelly as hard as the kids had.

CHAPTER 3

O f all the organizations Kelly had belonged to—business, civic, professional, and fraternal—the navy reserve center was the worst of the lot. They were the poorest managed, had the worst job attitudes, were often poorly led … He could go on. Kelly had always fought with unpaid berthing and travel claims. They had even failed to send up his security clearance applications.

It's like all of us reserves compete for limited staff administrative time, he had thought.

Many lower enlisted sailors had been cheated out of retirement points by upper ranking sailors getting their paperwork done ahead of junior people. Kelly was missing some past annual training points as well. He had turned in the record copies, but the staff always failed to accomplish anything.

If the senior enlisted and officers were prevented from having their paperwork completed until every junior sailor had theirs done …, Kelly often thought. But that was just wishful thinking.

Kelly and Gwen walked into the administration offices at a quarter after seven in the morning. There wasn't an admin sailor to be seen or heard. At a quarter to eight, the yeoman first class (YN1) and the personnel specialist third class (PS3) showed up in civilian clothes.

"MC1, do you have everything?" asked the yeoman.

"Yes, I'm ready to go," said Kelly.

"Well, have a seat. When we finish our physical training, we will start on your premobilization."

Gwen looked at Kelly as she wondered why they'd had to get there so early if all the staff was going to do was exercise. Kelly shook his head.

At eight fifteen, the skipper came in. He was a new reserve center commanding officer, just released from Iraq. Kelly had had his doubts about the new boss the first time he had seen him. Their last skipper was a very hard worker. Kelly hadn't lost a single retirement point during the two years he was on board, and his travel claims had all been paid before the government credit card company shut off the charge account.

The lieutenant commander grudgingly spoke to Kelly as he walked past and turned into his office.

He has never shaken my hand, thought Kelly.

A little before nine o'clock, the YN1 and the PS3 came back and started Kelly's paperwork. They went over his government life insurance and put in the new addresses for his kids, stepdaughter, and stepson. The PS3 had him write in all of the address changes in his page two, the record the military looked up if he was killed in action. The navy corpsman called him into the medical spaces and gave him his second anthrax shot. Then she checked over his record to make sure he was up-to-date on all his other shots.

Kelly walked back down to the administration office.

"YN1, am I flying out today?" he asked.

"Yes," the YN1 answered. "You'll leave late this afternoon."

"Would it be all right if Gwen drives me instead of riding in the navy van?"

The yeoman always jumped at those offers. It kept staff from having to drive mobilized sailors to the airport.

"Yes, you can do that. Just be sure you're there on time," said the YN1.

"Do you have the itinerary?" asked Kelly.

"It's here somewhere," the YN1 said as he fumbled through his desk drawers. Unable to find it, he finally spoke up. "We'll get it to you before we're done."

Gwen just shook her head when she heard that. *Everything Kelly has said about this place is true*, she thought.

Just before the staff shoved off for lunch at eleven fifteen, they got Kelly's paperwork completed and a new itinerary printed off. They never did find the original one.

"We're almost done," said the PS3. "Let me print off this new page two and have you sign it."

Kelly signed the copies, and she put the new set in his personnel record.

"Have you got your medical record?" asked the YN1.

"Right here," said Kelly.

"Well, here's your personnel record and all of your papers," said the yeoman. "And here is your itinerary. Your plane leaves at 1730 hours. Be sure you're there early."

"We will be, YN1. See you when I get back."

Kelly and Gwen headed for the door. They killed some time with lunch at the Kansas City, Kansas, racetrack shopping center, shopped a bit, and then headed for the airport.

Kansas City International, or properly called Mid-Continent International Airport, was on the Missouri side of the Kansas City area. The way the state line followed the Missouri river, they would actually drive straight north and even west a little bit, cross the river, and head to the airport located northwest of downtown.

Kelly pulled into the B terminal and parked in the standing only area to unload by the curb. Gwen stood with his bags while he moved the car into the ten-dollars-an-hour lot and walked back to carry the luggage inside.

The line was long at the airline counter, but Kelly didn't think it would take forever.

At check-in, the attendant looked down her nose at Kelly's seabags. It was obvious he was military, and she took them with no extra baggage charges. Kelly asked if Gwen could get a pass to go through security and see him onto the plane. The airline attendant said, "Sure," and processed both passes at the same time.

"I didn't check my purse before I came," said Gwen. "I don't think I have any knives or scissors."

Kelly didn't stop to help her look. After waiting in line again, he put his backpack, laptop, and shoes into separate bins and then emptied his pockets into a small items bowl. Gwen put her purse and shoes into a bin, and one by one they stepped through the metal detector.

His gate was close. They could see it just around the corner. Kelly began to get nervous as he saw the tension in Gwen's eyes. They held hands as they walked into the seating area together. They sat in the open chairs on the back row.

Kelly worried. Was everything done for Gwen while he was gone? He had finished all of the farm and house projects that spring. He had used his two-week navy training check to go through Gwen's car. He had spent $1,150 on new struts and two tires. She and the home should be in pretty good shape.

"I didn't get the lawn mower tires replaced," said Kelly.

"I know," said Gwen. "Be sure to air up the front left tire every time I mow and air up the right rear tire every other time."

"Guess I've repeated it often enough," laughed Kelly. "I'm in section two to board."

"I'm not going to cry," said Gwen.

"Is that right?" Kelly asked.

Gwen just smiled, looking away from her husband. This wouldn't be so hard if he was just going to a ship somewhere. It was the going to a war zone where American troops were killed almost every day that made the good-bye so hard.

The redheaded airline attendant walked briskly up to the counter. She laid her papers on top, walked up to the boarding gate, and quickly opened the tall door. Picking up the telephone, she pushed the number for the loudspeaker and then announced for the first-class and disabled passengers to board.

Both Kelly and Gwen nervously moved their legs. It was a few minutes before the next announcement.

"Now boarding zones one and two," said the attendant.

Gwen was already crying. Every emotion she had kept forced down all day began shoving its way to the top. Big tears streamed down her cheeks, and other passengers began to notice.

Kelly wasn't quite as emotional as Gwen, but like most men, the sight of a crying loved one welled his eyes too. They both stood up. He left his backpack in the seat next to him and hugged her hard. Gwen wrapped her arms around Kelly's neck like she wasn't going to let go.

"I love you, babe," said Kelly. "I'll be as safe as I can be and come back soon."

Gwen heard the phrase *safe as can be*. It didn't help much.

"I love you, Kelly," said Gwen. She let go of his neck, seeming to motion for him to leave the embrace and get on the plane.

He kissed her hard, and for a moment, time just stopped. All of their thoughts were on each other. The redheaded attendant had watched this so many times she couldn't remember how many. But this one touched her, and without her even realizing it, tears began to well up in her big green eyes.

Kelly turned and walked down the gateway. He handed his boarding pass to the emotional attendant, who was obviously mad at herself for not being more professional.

Gwen held her breath until he was out of sight. Then she sobbed aloud and was briefly comforted by nearby passengers and an attendant.

Gwen was mad at herself, too, for not keeping ahold of her emotions. She had managed to be stout until Kelly was out of sight. She didn't know where the loud sob had come from. She thanked the people who had come up to help. As soon as she saw Kelly's plane take off, she headed for the front of the airport. As she walked by the rows of seats, she decided it would be best to sit for a while. Gwen wasn't in emotional shape to drive, and she knew it.

Why did I have to cry out loud? thought Gwen. She collapsed into a seat and thoughts ran through her head.

I didn't want him to go, she repeated. *He never even asked me if it was all right, like it wasn't supposed to be up to me.*

Gwen thought for a minute. *There are probably thousands of wives and girlfriends who, like me, weren't asked if it was okay for their men to go either.* She knew he had been doing this long before she came along.

I wonder if it was Pat who told him it was okay to join the navy, she thought angrily. *That's the way to get rid of a husband you don't want.*

Gwen got up to go to the car. The airport's automatic door blew in the hundred-degree heat from outside. She walked to her car and looked hard at the gray Impala.

What if he doesn't come back? she said to herself.

Kelly was turning down the boarding gangway toward the plane door when he heard Gwen's sob. He stopped and took one step in her direction. The passengers and baggage attendants had heard it too.

No, thought Kelly. *That would be the wrong thing to do. She's probably mad at herself and I would just make it worse*. He turned back toward the plane and made himself step aboard.

Kelly didn't want to admit that if he had taken the second step toward Gwen, he might not have been able to go on to the war.

The plane didn't take long to board. It was only half-full, and the crew was obviously trying to stay on schedule. The attendant told the passengers to buckle up, and the pilot ordered the push back from the gate.

It was after midnight, thanks to typical connection delays, before Kelly got to his berthing at the bachelor enlisted quarters (BEQ) on Norfolk Navy Base in Virginia. He would have a short night.

CHAPTER 4

The next morning, Kelly reached for his phone to call Leigh. He usually woke up before the alarm went off, even if he had a short night. It rang just before he grabbed it. He looked to see if it was Leigh. It was.

"Hello there, Ensign Select," said Kelly.

"Just wanted to see if you wanted a ride," said Leigh. "I have a rental car."

Officers and senior enlisted were the only ones designated for cars this time, and Leigh qualified now with her ensign select status. He and Leigh had ridden together for exercises since they had come into the new public affairs unit two years ago.

"I could use the ride," said Kelly.

"Pick you up at 0615 hours," answered Leigh.

Kelly was standing outside the BEQ in his working white uniform when Leigh showed up in a blue mustang—her rental car.

"How did you get this?" asked a surprised Kelly.

"They were out of compacts again," said Leigh. "Darn shame."

The ride to the Joint Forces Command was forty minutes during rush hour. They had to go through the midtown tunnel.

"Are you ready for the desert?" asked Leigh

"I think so," said Kelly. "Gwen is having trouble. She hasn't been with a military man before."

"You don't know what trouble is," said Leigh. "Bill totally threw a fit."

"How bad?"

"He stopped talking to me for the first day. Then he left and I guess moped around and pouted. He didn't talk to me until Saturday, and then it was just to find out when I would fly out and how long I would be gone."

"You're right about having the harder spouse to deal with," said Kelly. "Gwen tried to hold it all in at the airport gate and then melted down when she thought I was out of earshot."

"Did you go back?" asked Leigh.

"Almost," said Kelly. "But I thought better of it."

"I think you did the right thing," said Leigh. "She didn't know you heard her. But if I knew my guy had heard me … Well, I would have been mad if you didn't come back."

"Point taken," said Kelly as he looked at her and grinned.

The JFCOM building looked large in the distance as Leigh turned down the drive past the lakes. Built to host secure military exercise scenarios, the large gray building had huge parking lots on all sides.

The gate check required an additional security clearance badge in addition to a military ID. Kelly had his *secret* level red one. He had some outstanding medical and credit card debt stemming from his divorce. His clearance had recently been reviewed very closely. Leigh had a *top secret* level blue one. She had never been divorced and dealt with children's medical insurance that didn't pay. She had squeaky clean financial history.

The security officer checked them both, and they went to the magnetic door card reader. Kelly swiped his and held the door for Leigh. They both walked down the passageway and went into the little meeting room. The black seats were built into a sloping theater design for group training, video conferences, and lecture presentations.

Like the rest of the building, the air-conditioning in this room was set very cold because of all the expensive computer equipment. All the sailors knew to bring their jackets, and everyone mobilized was there, including all the enlisted, chiefs, and officers.

"I think we all know why we're here," said Senior Chief Bonnie Wilson as she called the group to order. "Our unit, or most of us anyway, have been mobilized to central command at Al Asad Air Base in western Iraq. We will be relieving some of the personnel there and augmenting the command for some additional mission capabilities. Admiral Select Benton will brief us more."

"Attention on deck," shouted leading petty officer, LPO Harrison Wade.

Everyone in the unit stood to attention as the young dark-haired admiral (select) walked into the room.

"As you were," he said. "I'm sure you're all wondering what I'm doing here."

Admiral (selects) usually promoted into administrative duties. In this case, Benton would have promoted to a reserve rear admiral, in charge of key areas of navy reserve activities. Most wouldn't stay with a unit mobilizing for longer than a year.

"It took some talking," said the admiral, "but I'm going to stay a captain for a while longer and go with my shipmates. No way was I going to pass up going to theater." *In-theater* was a military term used to describe serving in a wartime area.

Benton went on to briefly say that the current admiral would stay in the same position for his deployment. Then a unit chief went over their training, uniform issue, and berthing. They would receive woodland camouflage for their coming field exercise (FEX) and be issued desert camouflage just prior to deploying.

They would complete small arms training at a nearby shooting facility, train for chemical, biological, and radiological on the Norfolk base, do IED avoidance at Little Creek Naval Amphibious Base, and complete a brief FEX at Camp Pershing in northern Virginia.

At the first break, Leigh leaned over to Kelly. "You ready for the field?"

"I can deal with the heat and camping," said Kelly. "It's the sleep deprivation that will be hard on me. I get short-tempered when I get my nights interrupted."

Leigh had some allergies. Kelly worried about her in the heat and dust at both training facilities. She was used to being in a TV station or at home in northern Ohio, not out in the southern heat to which Kelly was accustomed. He had spent days out in the sun on Gwen's farm. He had also worked a part-time job back in Sedalia every summer where he spent every evening and weekend in hot cornfields for years.

The public affairs unit completed their brief and headed back to their barracks. The next day would be very full, with classes, uniform issue, and gear assignment.

Later that day, they met in classrooms in the Norfolk Reserve Center. Their tasks consisted of administrative details and filling out forms. Next they completed some of the more pressing computer online courses, which took most of the afternoon.

The next day, the PAO group went to warehouses on the supply side of the main naval base. There they received their first set of uniforms, CBR packs, and gas masks.

That afternoon, they met back at the Norfolk Reserve Center for more specialized instruction on weapons code, shooting readiness, and rules of engagement. After lunch at the base galley, they were ready to head for the armory and sign up for their weapons.

"I haven't shot an M16 in forever," said Kelly.

"I learned on it in the army," said Leigh.

The sailors stood in a long line outside the armory. When the inner door opened, one member of the group rang the bell to be let in.

A godlike voice barked out through the opening door, "Get those backpacks and bicycles away from that fence. You can put everything across the street."

All of the sailors complied. As they came back across, the buzzer sounded and the whole group filed in and completed their weapon issue cards.

"I thought they were going to issue the guns," said Kelly.

"Well, they won't let you carry that around here," said Leigh. "You'll check it out to shoot and return it right back. In Iraq or 'in-theater' is when we'll carry them everywhere."

The sailors completed the paperwork and were assigned the M16s they would pick up the following morning.

Back at the classroom, the instructors notified the sailors

that they were getting the rest of the afternoon off. But they were expected back at the armory at 0500 the next day to check out their weapons and proceed to the shooting range.

"Bet I can outshoot you," said Leigh.

"You're on," answered Kelly.

It was dark as could be when the sailors assembled at the armory at 0450 hours. Most of them were wearing their blue shipboard dungarees. A few had their own woodland camouflage. Most of the sailors, including Leigh, had walked from the BEQ. Kelly rode his bicycle, as usual, with his front and rear lights shining brightly.

"We could see you coming a mile away," said one of the supply sailors as Kelly rode up.

"Good morning, Mr. Raines," said Leigh. "How in the world did you get that bicycle here?"

"I brought it down in my seabags."

Leigh couldn't imagine how he got that thing in a seabag.

"I guess you brought more than one seabag?" she asked.

Military luggage, even if it was overweight, was commonly shipped free. Many sailors didn't know that.

"That's right," said Kelly. "I brought three, including the flight bag."

Leigh just shook her head.

The sailors checked out their M16s and two magazine cartridges and waited for the bus. Soon they were on their way to the nearby shooting range.

"So much for breakfast," said one of the sailors.

"I brought mine," said another as he reached into his camouflage side pocket and pulled out some of the free breakfast biscuit sandwiches from the BEQ.

At the range, the sailors got the safety brief and the usual shooting instructions. They divided into three groups and prepared to start their shoot. Kelly and Leigh were in the third group.

The line was set up under a long unpainted awning similar to a porch built over a gray cement floor. The targets were glued onto brown cardboard backings in front of a large earthen berm to stop the bullets.

"Going to outshoot you there, MC1," said Leigh as she took her place by the thick post.

"We'll see about that, Ensign Select," said Kelly.

When the shooting began, Kelly struggled with his glasses. He hadn't shot since he had them made. Being a lefty shooter, he struggled with the safety and releases, which were all on the other side of the gun for right-handed shooters. On Gwen's Kansas farm, he had a shotgun and that was it. The only time he ever shot rifles was for the navy.

As the range instructors brought the targets in, Kelly didn't feel good about his coming score.

Leigh brought her target over to show Kelly as soon as the range instructor finished adding up the points. She had qualified with a 145 score. A 140 was the minimum military shooters had to make.

"How'd you do Kelly?" she asked.

"The worst I've ever done," said a frustrated Kelly. "I made a whole ninety-eight."

Leigh was very surprised Kelly hadn't shot better than her. He was usually very good at any type of athletic event. With such a large group, they were only allowed to shoot once. Anyone who didn't qualify was told to come back the next day. The bus ride back to base was a dismal one for Kelly.

"What did you shoot before?" Leigh asked.

"I shot expert in both rifle and pistol," said Kelly.

Leigh walked back to her room as Kelly unlocked his bike from the armory parking lot post and rode back to his BEQ.

On the phone that night, Kelly told Gwen about his day.

"I couldn't hit anything."

"I wonder why," said Gwen.

"I do too," said Kelly. "I always did well before, but I haven't shot a rifle since the last time for the navy and that was seven years ago."

Gwen paused before she answered. "On the farm, you shoot skeet without your glasses. Do you think that might have something to do with it?"

"Hadn't thought about it. I can see fine far away. But I have to be able to see the close in sight to line up with the one down the barrel."

"Well, I'm just the navy wife back home," said Gwen. "But I've watched you shoot here and that was how you did it."

Kelly thought about it all night.

The next morning, Kelly put his glasses in his pocket and toted his rifle onto the range with the other nonqualifiers. He was embarrassed to even be there with them.

I hope leaving these glasses off helps, he thought.

The range senior chief called the group together. "We're all going to battle-sight zero the rifles again," said the range senior chief. The BZO acronym stood for readjusting the gun sights for each shooter to try to help them hit their targets better.

We just did this yesterday, thought Kelly. *But if it's going to help, I'm ready to do it.*

Sure enough, Kelly's sights did change when he shot without glasses. The range assistant caught Kelly shooting that way and made him use a pair of no-correction safety glasses.

"If they fog up on you from the humidity, just push them down your nose and look over the top," whispered the assistant.

When the shooting started, Kelly did just that. Even though they weren't fogged yet, he pushed them down and looked over the tops.

"You're hitting a lot of black," said the range assistant. Black was navy speak for the bulls-eye.

When they went to score the target, Kelly was amazed that he had shot so much better.

"You have a 151," said the range assistant. "But we're going to shoot one more time. You should score higher."

Sure enough, Kelly did score higher. He felt confident, his breathing seemed natural, and he had the trigger slap down as well.

"This time you're hitting the black on the kneeling as well as the prone," said the assistant.

When they went to score the target, even the range master was impressed.

"You shot right up with me," he said. "This adds up to 176, qualifying you for expert."

Kelly was surprised to have done so well even though he had shot like that in the past.

At the muster before the group boarded the bus, the senior chief for the gun range addressed the group.

"I think you can see that the sight adjustments for your weapons helped several of you. And who is Raines?"

Kelly looked up and raised his hand. The sailors all looked in his direction.

"This guy went from a failing 98 to an expert 176!" said the range senior chief.

Back at the barracks, Kelly was hassled by his shipmates.

"Look at this guy. He takes off his glasses and outshoots everybody," said newly pinned Chief James Johnson.

Leigh was quick to come and congratulate Kelly.

"I outshot you for a day," said Leigh. "How did taking off your glasses help that much?"

"I guess because I'm farsighted, I didn't really need them for shooting."

"Well, I'm nearsighted. If I took mine off I wouldn't even see the target," said Leigh. "And next time we shoot, have Gwen give me advice so I can get the expert ribbon."

CHAPTER 5

Following the mini field exercise and a short weekend break, the sailors began their lockdown for the flight.

Kelly had stored his bicycle at a Virginia Beach chiropractor's office. Both he and Leigh had gone to the NAS post office and sent everything back home that they weren't taking overseas.

The base movie theater became the location for the sailors and a Seabee detachment. They were all given time to call home one last time, and then they boarded the plane for their long flight from Naval Air Station Oceana in Virginia Beach near Norfolk.

Following a brief stopover in Germany, the group landed in Kuwait. It was an almost twelve-hour flight. It was going on midnight Kuwait time when they got off the plane and helped sort their luggage.

The bus ride to their camp in Kuwait wasn't far. Camp Moreell was an in-processing type of facility to get troops accustomed to the new military "war-theater" life they would be leading. They would also go through the same camp on their way home. Everyone was assigned a battle buddy with whom they would have to go everywhere, along with their guns.

"You going to go everywhere I want to go, Mr. Raines?" asked Leigh.

"I would be glad to," said Kelly. "As long as you don't get me up for middle-of-the-night head calls."

"We've already talked about it," said Leigh. "Senior says that we can use other women for heads and showers. But you have to be my battle buddy for galley and exchange trips."

The bus pulled into the camp and, after the ID check, proceeded to the barracks area. As soon as it stopped, the sailors didn't wait to be told to unload the baggage. They just formed a line at the baggage door and started passing green seabags and flight bags out.

"Gather around for your berthing assignments," said Wilson.

The sailors were berthed sixteen people to each Southwest Asia hut, or SWA-hut. The buildings were thirty-two feet long with sixteen bunk beds inside. They also had shelves built into the wall right by the top bunks. All of them were air-conditioned.

"I hope we get nicer quarters than this in Iraq," said Leigh.

"Me too," said Kelly. "Guys will be getting up at all hours for watches. I sure don't want to be sleeping with sixteen of them."

"We will have quarters at 1030 hours," said Senior Chief Wilson. "Get some sleep and meet in this same area."

The sailors brought their gear and baggage into their SWA-huts. No one needed to be told to go to bed. Most just unpacked enough to get onto the bunks and crashed.

The next morning, a few sailors went to breakfast. Most slept until their alarms went off and then got dressed for the ten-thirty muster.

Kelly trudged out of bed early, threw his gym shorts and T-shirt on, and headed for the showers. He washed, shaved, and headed back to dress in his SWA-hut. When he opened the door, he couldn't recognize which bunk was his. Sailors had clothes and open bags everywhere. He finally picked his out and added to the mess.

The sailors were already assembling when he saw Leigh standing with the other women.

"Good morning, Mrs. Andrews," said Kelly.

"Good morning to you, Mr. Raines," said Leigh. "How was your night?"

"Not exactly a long peaceful slumber," said Kelly. "But I did get some rest."

Senior Chief Wilson walked to the front. Since the skipper

wasn't there, the LPO didn't assemble the sailors into ranks. The public affairs contingent quieted as she got ready to speak.

"We're going to be here for several days," said Senior Chief Wilson. "We will have classes on preliminary marksmanship instruction PMI and go the shooting range. We will also receive our modular tactical vests, MTV and small arms protective inserts, and SAPI plates."

She went on to describe their dress codes, weapon rules and liberal morale, welfare and recreation, and MWR times. "We won't do anything in the evenings here. Those are free time for you. Remember, your weapons go with you everywhere," said Wilson. "Meet back here at 1300. We may begin our gear issue."

Kelly and Leigh had some time to kill, so they walked to the base MWR building.

"Here's the phone bank," Leigh said. "We can call home late evenings or early mornings. That will be the early morning or evening times back home."

"I called Gwen from Germany," Kelly said. "But I bet she would like to hear from me again tonight."

"Bill is getting a little better about me being gone," Leigh said.

The two looked around at the MWR game room, library, and basic amenities the small base camp had to offer.

"Take me to lunch, battle buddy," Leigh said.

That afternoon the sailors were issued their MTV protective equipment. They shot rifles and pistols at the range in full gear. Everyone struggled to hit anything wearing the weight of the vests.

"Can you even hold your rifle?" Leigh asked Kelly.

"I can hold it up," he said, "but it's hard to hold the barrel still."

The heat began to get to everyone. Wearing the MTV vest and standing in the blazing hot sun soon had all of the sailors feeling the effects of dehydration.

"I just want to get this off," said Kelly as the group finished the last of their shooting training.

Before they began to walk off the range, many sailors—including Kelly—hoisted their vests over their heads and set them on the ground. Feeling the air blow through the sweat-soaked military blouses felt amazing.

"That's a lot better," Kelly said. "You takin' yours off?" he asked Leigh.

As she struggled to raise it, Kelly grabbed it by the back handle and whisked it over her head. Leigh had her doubts about if this was a good idea.

"They said it is easier to wear them than to carry them," she said. "I don't think I can carry mine. I'll have to put it back on."

"You've got a big strong shipmate here," Kelly reminded her.

Leigh wasn't about to walk back like a "girl," so when they were ordered back to the buses, she carried her vest just like everybody else. But Kelly knew Leigh and knew she would let him help her if he was patient.

Soon she was really struggling to walk with her vest. He reached a strong arm down and grabbed ahold of one side of her vest's back strap. She looked up at him with her big eyes and gave him an unspoken thank-you. He looked right back at her, his very best friend and shipmate.

Soon bigger sailors were helping other strength-challenged shipmates, sharing their MTV vest-carrying loads.

Kelly and Leigh's last day at Camp Moreell was a Sunday. They walked to the base chapel that morning and spent the rest of the day together. Both of them cared deeply about the other, but there was no crossing of the affection line. They were both married, and they knew and respected that fact.

As dedicated as they were to their marriages, it was also true that their feelings for each other were very strong, a lot stronger than either of them realized. But they could resist their temptation to go further, as long as nothing pushed them in that direction.

Leigh and Kelly walked together to the phone bank to call home to their spouses, Bill and Gwen.

Following supper at the DFAC, they took all of their stuff out to load onto the waiting buses. They would fly at night again, on their last travel leg to Iraq.

The ride to the airfield from Camp Morrell was short. An

air force C-17 was waiting to take them into Iraq. The contingent of Seabees and public affairs sailors were met by a contingent of soldiers and several assorted marines. Kellogg, Brown, and Root KBR civilians were at the airport parking ramp waiting to go as well. The KBR people were civilian workers hired to help staff the military bases and do work not assigned to military members.

The group formed working parties to load their baggage onto pallets. In-theater military took over from there. They used forklift trucks to pick up the net-covered pallets and put them onto the plane. A C-17 was large enough to load the luggage first and have the troops walk by the cargo area to their seats, which faced sideways rather than forward like civilian planes.

Everyone had to wear their MTV vests. They were allowed to carry on one backpack and their guns. Many had cameras strapped to their necks. On the plane, several people ignored the no photograph signs and took pictures of everything.

They left well after dark, complying with security requirements for all large planes taking off and landing in Iraq.

The large air force C-17 circled the Al-Asad Air Base for its approach. Large planes risked surface-to-air missile attacks when they came in with long descents and approaches, so the pilots circled to descend rather than make the typical straight-line descent they would do in a safer area. The plane bounced as the wheels touched down.

Hydraulic sounds of the rear ramp being lowered echoed through the plane. The passengers could see the bright lights and dull gray runway of the airbase in western Iraq.

Similar to the American Southwest, Iraq had rolling hills of treeless landscape dotted with small bushes and desert plants. The Al Asad Air Base was built on a more level part of the dry land area. The large runway was the flattest spot for miles.

A marine dressed in a reflective jacket and large ear protectors walked up from outside. "May I have your attention please," said the marine. "You all need to grab your gear and line up behind me on the runway. When we're ready to go, I will escort you to the

AACG-DACG (Airlift Arrival Control Group-Departure Airlift Control Group) building."

Everyone followed the marine off the aircraft and lined up in two lines. They would have to cross uneven ground between the runway and the parking ramp. At a pace faster than many of the group could manage, particularly at night, they walked in quick-time toward the buildings.

Kelly was the second one in the right line. Leigh was right behind him. As they double-timed across the runway and onto the Iraqi desert between the runway and parking ramp, Kelly felt that they were going too fast for some of his shipmates.

Halfway across, Kelly finally spoke out to the marine. "Hey, shipmate, we need to slow down. A lot of these people aren't in shape to keep up this pace."

The marine turned and looked at Kelly. He didn't answer but grudgingly slowed down, a bit anyway. Kelly looked at Leigh and the others behind him. The lines were stretched out way back, with long gaps in several areas.

As they completed the four-minute walk—which could have been safely done in seven or eight minutes—they crossed the parking ramp and entered through the doors of the AACG-DACG building. Sailors, soldiers, and Seabees all filed in over the next several minutes. Two Seabees helped one female soldier who had obviously sprained her ankle in one of the holes the group had come across at night.

An obviously upset army staff sergeant spoke out loudly as he came through the doors. "Where the fuck is the marine who marched this group?" he demanded.

"He went in those doors there," said Kelly. "He told us to wait here and he would come back for our IDs."

When the marine came back, a typical ass-chewing took place between the army staff sergeant and the marine corporal.

"We had people falling in holes all the way back to the runway," said the army sergeant. "What were you even thinking marching us at double-time over uneven ground at night?"

"Just getting you away from the runway so the plane can take off," said the corporal, "and following orders."

"I don't care what your orders say," said the army staff sergeant. "That was way too fast, unsafe, and now we have several people hurt!"

The marine corporal had been gathering ID cards the whole time the army staff sergeant was yelling at him. Like most military confrontations, nothing much ever came out of a shouting match, even when one side was clearly right.

Following the arrival at the AACG-DACG, the group divided into their respective military groups. Buses soon began arriving to take each branch of service to their respective berthing locations around the base.

The marines were headed to the east side, soldiers to the north, and sailors and Seabees to the west. They would stay in cans, or small house trailer types of temporary dwellings. They would stay two people to a can, with beds that could bunk up if the residents so desired.

"No more tents," said Senior Chief Wilson. "Everyone will have heat and air-conditioning."

As the bus pulled into the can area, everyone noticed the high cement T-walls. These were large barriers to help deter indirect fire from mortar attacks, which meant a shot that was fired up in the air to come down in an arc onto an enemy force. Al Asad had been a tempting target for indirect mortar attacks in the past. Just prior to the new arrivals coming, the military had moved the protective fences farther out to help deter the insurgent mortar attacks.

Kelly grabbed his bags as he got off the bus. He would be sharing a room with a marine religious program specialist RP assigned to the Seabees. Leigh would be sharing with a female navy storekeeper SK also assigned to the Seabees. When she received her commission, she would move into a can by herself.

Unpacking didn't take long. The sailors had sent many of their things forward in the mail. It would be weeks before all of that arrived.

Kelly and the other sailors went to bed. They would be able to sleep for the few hours left in the night.

CHAPTER 6

W hen his alarm went off at 0530, Kelly trudged to the men's showers.

It's a lot like being in college again, he thought. Kelly's days at the University of Missouri dormitories had been like this. Only the military showers and heads weren't just down the hall; troops had to walk to a different building.

After dressing, Kelly knocked on Leigh's door to see if she wanted to go to breakfast.

"You hungry?" he said as she opened the door.

"Yep," she said. "Is the RP going?"

"He's still setting up his stuff," said Kelly.

They walked to the bus stop and waited with several public affairs sailors and Seabees. The bus pulled up a short time later, and the group was off toward the DFAC. They stopped several more times on the route, letting off and picking up servicemen and women along the way.

The Al Asad DFACs were a lot like the ones at Camp Moreell, only they were bigger and there were more of them. They were also very far away.

"We're going to have to ride the bus everywhere," said Leigh. "At least I will. How long before you have a bicycle, Kelly?"

"As soon as I can get to the exchange," he said.

After breakfast, the public affairs sailors headed for the PAO offices. Senior Chief Wilson assigned each MC to a desk. She also did assignment for computers, even though there were no computers there yet. As MCs, they would be required to write, Photoshop their pictures, and edit copy for less experienced MCs.

Their mission was to tell the story of what the American military was doing in the Middle East, to put the efforts in a positive light, and to gain political support on the home front.

Leigh and Kelly were together with two other MCs in a small office. Extension cords and computer cables were all over the place. There was one window.

Captain Benton met with the PAO group late in the morning.

"We have a lot of activities to cover," he said. "Who's not set up on the marine computer system?"

"No one is," said the senior chief. "The marine support staff will be here tomorrow to complete all of that."

In the afternoon, the captain gave the group the rest of the day off.

Kelly and Leigh headed straight for the exchange. New bicycles were lined up behind the cash registers. From blue and silver German bicycles to desert camouflage styles—they were all there to pick from. The military could get better prices and shipping from European cycling manufacturers than American bike suppliers.

The German bikes had different sized tire valve air fittings, but they weren't a lot different from bikes sold in the US. The store had a German hand air pump Kelly could use to air the tires up enough to ride to an electric air compressor pump.

"I've never had a German bike," Kelly said. "You going to get one, Leigh?" he asked.

"I don't think so," she said. "You go ahead and ride all you want, though."

Leigh was tight with her money. She had never spent much on extra things. Kelly was the adventurous one.

Leigh shook her head as Kelly paid more than two hundred dollars for the bike. All she bought were a few things for her room. Once outside, Kelly realized he didn't have his bike helmet or reflective vest. They were still in shipment.

"You going to take it on the bus?" Leigh asked him.

"The passageway is too narrow," he said. "I'll have to walk it. If

I dare ride it without my safety equipment, I take my chances getting pulled over by the MPs (army military police)."

"I'll walk with you," Leigh said.

Kelly spent the rest of the afternoon getting his bicycle ready to ride. He borrowed tools from the Seabees and adjusted the seat and handlebars for a tall rider. Next, he reset all of the brake adjustments and gear settings.

This thing just barely goes into first gear, he said to himself.

He dug his issue helmet and running reflective belt out of his seabags. Since none of his shipped items had arrived yet, he would have to wear his military helmet and his reflective running belt to pass the bike safety regulations. He could carry his M16 on his back with the three-point sling.

This should get me past the MPs, he thought.

Next he pedaled over to the civilian KBR camp to see if their air compressor had European sized valve stem fittings. Bicycle tires lasted longer if they were kept filled to the maximum air pressure. His hand pump would only get the tires to forty pounds.

Beside the KBR air compressor was a metal box with several size adapters, including the German size Kelly needed. He could take the tires to the full sixty-pound maximum.

Leigh and several other women were outside when he rode back into camp.

"You look kind of dangerous there, Mr. Raines," said Leigh as he rode up.

"Wait till my bike helmet and reflective vest finally get here," he said. "Then I can lose some of this tactical effect."

Leigh and Kelly spent the rest of the week setting up their desks and getting familiar with the base. The closest DFAC was number one. It was half a mile away. The exchange was within walking distance from there. So was the post office, gym, and combined faiths building, or church.

The days started early. Kelly was up at 0530 every morning. He liked to eat breakfast, and his early start gave him time to make the DFAC shortly after it opened. He had just enough time to pedal back to the office by seven in the morning.

The PAO sailors were allowed liberal exercise time. Kelly liked to do his push-ups, pull-ups, and sit-ups at noon. He would head for the gym on his way to lunch. That left his afternoons free to run, bike, or swim at Saddam Hussein's pool before evening dinner.

Leigh didn't care anything about an early breakfast. She kept snacks in her room and most of the time just took one to work with her. She rode the bus everywhere.

She exercised every other day. All she did was run and lift weights, usually in the afternoon. When it was Kelly's run day, she would jog with him.

She and Kelly organized a PAO Bible study group. They met on Wednesday evenings. Kelly had found a choir to sing with at the Catholic service, and he regularly went to their Sunday morning mass. He especially liked their musicians, including a violinist, clarinet player, and guitarist. The Catholic piano player was exceptional. There was no organ.

Leigh cared nothing about going to Catholic mass, but the Protestant service started later than Kelly's. So on many Sundays, she would just go to worship with Kelly.

"His choir is very good," she had told her storekeeper roommate. "They even have violin solos!"

Her Protestant service had two guitarists and a drummer that played Christian rock. There was no choir.

After two weeks, the PAO skipper began to schedule press assignments. The Seabees were beginning their building schedule and would be putting up forward operating bases and combat outposts (FOBs and COPs) for the marines. It presented an excellent story and photo opportunity.

The convoy groups were all up and running, and new drivers were familiar with the various roads.

"Would all of you MCs come in here please?" said Senior Chief Wilson. "We're going to start working outside the wire."

Wilson gave out several press assignments. Leigh and Kelly were assigned to cover a new COP being built near Anah. They would go out with that evening's convoy and stay for two days.

"Pack your sleeping bags and a change of clothes," said Wilson. "The Seabees will transport all of the MREs for you."

Kelly went back to pack his stuff. They would have time to go to supper before the Seabee convoy picked them up at the PAO building at 2000 hours (8:00 p.m.).

After supper, Kelly carried his seabag and backpack to the bus stop. With his sleeping bag, he couldn't quite carry everything for an overnight trip on the bicycle. But he would leave it and other things at his office for following convoys.

Soon the loud Humvees and trucks showed up. Leigh and Kelly were assigned to the second Humvee. They loaded their stuff, put on their MTV gear, and climbed in.

The ride out was a long one. The convoys had hit several IEDs in the past month. They would go the long way around several hot spots in order to guarantee the safest transportation possible.

It was around 0230 hours when the group pulled into the new COP area. The lead vehicle stopped at the entry control point (ECP). Soon the marine watch standers motioned the rest of the Humvees and trucks in.

Leigh and Kelly were led to a tent where they could bed down for the rest of the night.

They would share a tent with some of the convoy drivers. She was the only woman at the new COP. Both Kelly and Leigh slept with their clothes on. It would only be a two-hour sleep.

The next day they ate an MRE breakfast.

"This isn't so bad," said Leigh as she opened her heat pouch.

Kelly looked at his shipmate.

"They're not so good either, at least the breakfast ones."

That morning they took pictures of everything. The Seabee builders were setting up HESCOS—big wire and cloth enclosed containers the Seabee equipment operators would fill with dirt and rocks.

After shooting those, the photographers turned their attention to the carpentry work. Kelly got a good shot of the builders putting up trusses.

They finished the day with pictures of the construction

electricians wiring up one of the buildings. It was close to the work area quitting time of 1800.

The marine guard detail patrolled the perimeter. None of the Seabees or the MCs were assigned a watch. As long as the Seabees were building them an outpost, the marines would take care of security.

Leigh and Kelly looked forward to getting a better night's sleep. They used a common privacy divider to change clothes behind. It was just after eight when they crawled into their sleeping bags.

"Good night, Mrs. Andrews," said Kelly as he grinned in her direction.

"Good night, Mr. Raines," laughed Leigh.

The next day, Leigh and Kelly shot more pictures, mostly of the same things they had shot the day before. Kelly got some more quotes for the stories.

It's good to have some extra ones, he thought. *This way I can pick the best ones for the story.*

They would be leaving with an afternoon convoy for the trip back to the base.

Just after ten in the morning, the brief sound of an incoming rocket broke the beautiful morning.

Several marines and Seabees hollered out a warning, and everyone, including Kelly and Leigh, hit the deck and covered their ears. By instruction, all of the sailors were required to stay in that position for two minutes.

The rocket exploded fifty yards away from where the Seabee construction was taking place. After the two-minute time was up, everyone headed for the IDF bunkers, which were large cement coverings designed for indirect fire attacks.

Leigh and Kelly stayed inside with the Seabees and marines until the all clear was issued and accountability procedures began. Every sailor had to be documented as a survivor or victim. In this case, there had been only one rocket and no one was injured.

It was the first time Leigh and Kelly had been involved in hostile fire.

"Well, Mr. Raines," said Leigh, "are you glad you decided to be a sailor now?"

Kelly was dusting off his uniform just like Leigh was. "I sure wish I could shoot back," he said, "and I hope our perimeter patrols can find the guys."

Other personnel at the COP who had bit the dust several times over the past weeks seemed to take the rocket attack in stride. Leigh and Kelly didn't know that previous rockets had hurt several COP workers and killed one. A complete accounting of all military personnel took place, and after just over an hour, the construction site returned to normal busy activity.

Lunch consisted of more MREs and bottled water. They had some time to kill, so the two sailors talked about what they were going to do when they got back home.

"What are you going to spend your deployment pay on?" Kelly asked Leigh.

"I'm going to save it," said Leigh. "Bill and I might buy a new house on the west side of Columbus."

"I'm going to get a new planter," Kelly said. "I have my eyes on a Great Plains no-till drill."

"What in the world does a drill plant?" asked Leigh.

"It plants any small seed you want," Kelly replied. "Mostly I will use it to no-till in beans and wheat."

"Well, Farmer Brown," Leigh said, "I hope you and Gwen like your new planter. Does she want that as much as you do?"

"Nope," Kelly replied. "She wants to get a new car."

"Well, get her a car then," Leigh said. "How much is this no-whatever drill?"

"It's fourteen thousand dollars," he said. "I don't think we can buy a brand new car too."

"Well, I'm just the shipmate friend," Leigh said. "But if Gwen wants something, I would try to find a way to get it for her."

"I'll think about it," Kelly said. "I need a planter, though. It's really not a toy. It would be for work on the farm."

"Oh, now I see," Leigh replied. "Boy toys are actual necessities."

Kelly laughed aloud. "Well, it will be fun to use," he said. "But

I bet if Bill had a farm, he would want to have good equipment, or 'boy toys,' too."

At 1400 hours (2 p.m.), the convoy showed up. Some of the truck teams had stayed and were now in line with the Humvee security teams.

"It's good to get a day trip back," said Leigh.

"You betcha," agreed Kelly. "We lose enough sleep as it is."

It was 1930 hours when the convoy rolled back into Al Asad. The drivers had taken a somewhat faster way back to camp. Kelly and Leigh got out of their Humvee at the PAO building and took off their MTV vests. Their uniforms were wet with sweat.

"We don't have time to shower if we're going to make the DFAC before eight thirty," said Kelly, forgetting that Leigh was a woman for a bit.

"I am not going to dinner like this," she insisted. "We can go to the restaurant stands by the exchange. They are open later."

The sailors went to their cans and showered. They felt much better to be clean and dry. Then they walked to the Pizza Hajji Shop and gorged on thick crust Canadian bacon pizza.

CHAPTER 7

Kelly and Leigh had been back in their routine "in camp" life for a few days when the senior chief walked back to their office early one morning and shut the door.

"I want you two to go back to your cans and get your CBR packs and gas masks," she said, talking quietly. "Get your camera gear all ready to go and pack extra batteries and flash cards."

Leigh and Kelly looked at each other with anticipation. They knew this order wasn't ordinary.

As the senior chief reached for the door, she turned and spoke quietly again. "Not a peep about this, even if someone else has a high clearance. This mission is classified as a need-to-know basis only."

"Yes, Senior," said Kelly. Leigh also agreed.

Leigh had to wait for the bus to take her to her sleeping quarters. Kelly hopped on his bicycle. Since he could get around faster than Leigh, Kelly thought he might pack a little better for the coming trip. He could hardly believe they were going to actually use their CBR gear. All of the sailors had told him that he'd carry it over and back and never touch it.

Kelly suspected that some type of suspicious chemical weapons had been found. If that turned out to be true, this was the first he had heard of.

He changed into the worst uniform he had. It was clean, but it had some deep stains, tears, and wear marks. He grabbed some snacks to eat on the way and pedaled back to the PAO building.

Leigh wouldn't show up for another half hour, waiting for the bus. So Kelly gathered all the camera equipment they would need and the extra batteries. He had the camera bag all packed when she showed up.

"I thought you might get that all ready for us," she said. "I think we should take the video camera too."

Kelly hadn't thought of that.

"We might carry it all the way out there and they won't want it," he said.

"Trust me," Leigh said. "They will want it."

Both sailors grabbed their MTV vests, helmets, and gear. With the CBR backpacks and gas masks, they had to make two trips to get everything out to the quarterdeck.

They were waiting when the senior chief and the skipper showed up with just as much stuff.

"Step into the office," said Benton. He waited for Kelly, Leigh, and Wilson to get inside, and then he shut the door.

"It looks like some marines have found some of Saddam Hussein's weapons of mass destruction," Benton said. "I took a secure call a while ago for a camera crew request."

Leigh and Kelly looked at each other, thinking this would be a history-making discovery. They didn't know that other small stashes had already been found in other parts of Iraq.

"Kelly, you don't have a top-secret rating," Benton said. "But I need my best photographer on this one, so I am vouching for you."

Kelly was very proud to have his skipper ask for him.

Benton knew he had to give the bad news on their unit's new camera equipment.

"We've been ordered to sacrifice some of our better equipment," he said. "Bring the Canon 5-D. We won't be able to replace anything. You will have to use your own stuff for the rest of the deployment."

Kelly hated to give up the 5-D. But orders were orders.

"I have been reminded that this mission is of the highest security," Benton said. "Absolutely none of this can get out. I've been told these are orders from the president himself."

Kelly wondered why the administration wouldn't want to show

this to the world. President Bush had staked his political future on WMDs as a reason to go to war.

Kelly repacked the camera equipment bag so they would only use what the skipper had ordered and leave the rest. He also left one video camera packed, since he now agreed with Leigh that someone would want video where they were going.

A marine convoy pulled up to the PAO building, and the sailors loaded into the waiting Humvees. Benton and Wilson got into the third vehicle, and Leigh and Kelly were directed into the fourth. A two-star marine general would be leading the group. He didn't get out to welcome the PAO crew.

The convoy headed northwest toward Haditha. Here, the landscape opened up to more flatland, especially along the Euphrates River. Stark, bleak desert landscape changed to green and colorful beauty as they drove along the large river. Palm trees, wildflowers, and wheat and barley fields were prevalent along the river valley.

As they neared the dam, the convoy took a sharp left and went straight west along a narrow road that was more like a livestock path.

A very strong checkpoint was set up, manned by a full gate crew of marines in desert camouflage and full MTV gear. Kelly noticed that their weapons were all in condition three, with magazines loaded.

A .50-caliber machine gun emplacement was very evident to approaching vehicles.

The general was ready for the close ID check of all vehicle occupants. He handed a set of preapproved orders for the crew, complete with ID and picture copies, so that the marine watch standers could eye each vehicle occupant and cross-check each ID sheet.

Next they drove for less than a mile before approaching a second gate, where a less formal ID was conducted.

Once through that gate, they saw the fenced containment area. Rolls of concertina wire, with visible military contamination signs were prominently displayed.

A navy Seabee detachment sign was set up near a large tent.

Parked by the side of a large hole was a big track hoe, a bulldozer, and various other heavy pieces of construction equipment.

What looked like a large slab of cement had been set to the side of a below-ground storage bunker. Gray cement walls and steps led down into the belowground structure. Troops with full CBR suits were working inside.

The convoy pulled up to a large tent set up away from the project and behind the Seabee tent. The PAO contingent went inside, following the marine general.

"Captain Benton, would you and your people wait in the conference area?" said the general. "I will go get the on-scene commander and come and meet with you."

Kelly and Leigh sat in folding chairs set up around a temporary plywood table.

"I will see if we can use this area for our temporary office," said Benton. "We need to have computers brought in."

Soon the general was back with the on-scene commander, Marine Colonel Jon Grant. Tall and with a dark complexion from many hours in the Middle Eastern sun, the military manner of the seasoned officer showed as he welcomed the sailor contingent.

"We're glad you could come," said Grant. "We should have had you filming and photographing days ago."

"General, we need a place to work," said Benton. "I don't see any office space set up. Could we use this boardroom table?"

"Yes," Grant said. "But we don't have any computers to spare."

"We have ours," Benton said. "But whichever one we use, won't that stay with the flashcards as classified equipment?"

The general realized he hadn't thought of something. If he wanted the pictures Photoshopped, he would have to confiscate a navy laptop.

"And how about card readers?" questioned Benton.

Leigh and Kelly hadn't thought of the classified picture problem either. Kelly had the most up-to-date Photoshop program. But he had many personal and unit items on his laptop too.

Senior Chief Wilson spoke up next. "I have one of the newest laptops," she said. "I haven't put very much from my old computer on it yet. Let's put the Photoshop program on it and then leave it here. Kelly, have you still got more downloads available from your Photoshop CD?"

"Yes," he said. "I keep it in my backpack for occasions such as this."

"Donate your card reader too," Wilson directed. "Skipper and I can replace it with unit funds."

The marine general was happy with the agreement. "Then we're settled," he said. "Let's see if we can get everything shot today."

Kelly plugged in the USB cable for his CD download of Photoshop onto the senior chief's computer. He left it running. A marine would come get it when the software download was complete. He would take it to the location where the flash card download was to be done.

The makeshift project area had no nearby berthing available. The marines had been stationing night watches as the staff and workers went back to Al Asad every evening.

The PAO group put on their CBR equipment, even the skipper and senior chief. The marines would carry their everyday boots to the location where they would leave their suits following decontamination.

They walked out of the tent and toward the concertina wire enclosure. Another marine checkpoint was set up. The group provided their documentation, put on their hoods and gas masks, and proceeded toward the next checkpoint, where marine guards stood in full CBR gear.

No IDs were checked here, as the marines' only duty was to make sure entering parties had their gear on correctly. They were meticulous as they checked for gloves and exposed skin and made sure pant legs were securely fastened.

The group proceeded toward the dirt ramp and then headed down into the large hole and bunker opening.

Leigh and Kelly were sweating profusely inside their suits. Kelly had anticipated that and had not worn his glasses so he could still see. He would have to rely on the auto-focus camera setting to take his shots and hope for the best.

At the bunker, the group picked up an escort they guessed was a marine. It was hard to tell with the CBR suit on. They proceeded down inside.

Engineers had set up good lighting; Kelly was glad for that. He began to shoot as soon as they entered the area. Leigh had ended up with the video camera, and she did the same thing.

Other CBR equipped marines and soldiers showed up and opened temporary storage lockers, where the group saw what looked like plain military shells, about a foot or longer.

The obviously very old and discolored shells looked like something from World War I.

This isn't new weapons grade chemical ordinance, thought Kelly as he continued to shoot. *This is old stuff leftover from who knows how long ago.*

The marine escort said the mustard gas was in several containers and added that others had tested positive for sarin.

The Iraqis had not set up any type of proper chemical weapon storage.

They picked out a bunker and haphazardly stuck these old shells full of chemical in here, Kelly thought. He wondered how many Iraqi soldiers were burned or made sick from improperly handling this stuff.

Leigh took video of everything Kelly was shooting.

A temporary air-conditioning system had been set up in part of the bunker. Even though the bunker was open on both ends, the slightly cooler temperatures made wearing the suits much more bearable.

All in all, they saw about fifty old military shells filled with mustard gas and some sarin gas.

Woo-hoo, thought the PAO sailors. *So much for the vaunted weapons of mass destruction.* The same thing had been true at some other locations around Iraq and had been kept classified and out of the press.

The crew worked for almost three hours before calling it good. Changing flash cards, film tapes, and batteries hadn't been easy while wearing the gear and gloves.

As they came back up and out of the bunker, the general led them to a different area to exit. "I know you are thinking this chemical weapon find isn't such a big thing," he said. "But every shell you photographed was a WMD. The find is very important to our chain of command."

Benton wanted to ensure the safety of his team. "We are going to have to decontaminate as thoroughly as possible," he said. "We don't want to open the flashcard and video tape bags."

"We're aware of that too, sir," said a member of the marine wash team. "You will test it at the next tent."

Kelly and Leigh took out the cameras, and the wash team carefully wiped the 5-D and video recorder down with premoistened bleach wipes.

They could still be used, Kelly thought. *I will miss my Canon 5-D.*

The team headed out of the tent, up another ramp, and then through another CBR checkpoint gate. The CBR watch standers were like those at the first one, except they were using metering devices to check for the presence of mustard and sarin gases.

The crew entered the second tent. Kelly handed his camera to a CBR-clad marine. The marine opened the camera flash card door, and another marine struggled with his gloves to get the flash card out and then placed it into a Ziploc bag.

The process was repeated with Leigh's video camera and film tape.

Kelly and Leigh handed all of their full flash cards and tapes to the marines.

"Please be careful with these," Kelly said. "We don't want to have to reshoot this again."

"I'm sure you don't," said the CBR watch stander.

The marine carefully used a CBR metering device and went over the flash cards and videotapes. The device measured safe on both opened bags.

"You have to leave the rest of your gear here," the marine said.

Kelly handed him the camera. Leigh did the same with the video camera. They then went out of the area and into another tent, where they stripped out of their CBR gear and placed it in the receptacles provided.

Big wash stations were also set up, so the PAO crew scrubbed down their hands, faces, and necks. Showers were available too, but they would have had to put their sweaty uniforms back on. The crew waited to shower and change uniforms until they returned to Al Asad.

The sailors were each provided with cleaned, bagged replacement CBR packs and cleaned gas masks, all in the proper sizes. They put their everyday boots back on.

The PAO team carried everything back to the command tent where they had started. Both marine commanding officers were waiting for them.

"Are we going to get to see our pictures?" asked Kelly.

The two-star general was quick with his reply. "The CBR team will bring them over soon," he said. "But they are placing them into the chief's computer with medical gloves," he said. "You have to wear them too, for your Photoshop work."

A marine staff aid handed a box of extra-large medical gloves to Kelly.

Soon a marine came in with senior's computer. He had left the flashcards and readers in the decontamination area. All of the pictures were dropped into one huge file marked *blank*.

Kelly went to work on the first photo to pop up.

"Don't delete anything," the general said. "Keep the originals and rename each selected photo into a second file."

"Yes, sir," said Kelly.

The general, Benton, and Wilson looked at each photo as Kelly cropped, color corrected, and brightened the better ones to the highest possible clarity.

Kelly and the team spent three hours going through the photos. The decision was made not to do any editing with the videotapes.

"We are going to send all of the tapes to Washington," the general said. "They can properly handle them there."

Kelly saved the photo files onto a marine secure external hard drive, logged off the computer, and handed all of the equipment to the staff aide.

"Very good," said the general. "Captain Benton, I appreciate you bringing your crew here. And may I say it was a job very well done."

"Thank you, sir," said the skipper.

Benton didn't salute, as they were inside the tent. He asked his sailors to put on their MTV vests.

It was late afternoon as they carried their new CBR packs and empty camera bags out of the tent and climbed into their MTVR vehicles for the short ride back to the base. They would make it back in time for supper, which sounded pretty good as everyone had worked through their lunch time.

CHAPTER 8

L eigh's paperwork for commissioning had arrived while she was on the COP assignment with Kelly and were delayed a bit longer when they received the WMD orders. When she reported for work the next morning, Captain Benton called her into his office.

"Well, MC1, your paperwork for commissioning arrived. Truthfully, we've had it for a few days, but we have time to do it now. We want to put your ensign bars on this afternoon. Senior Chief and I have arranged a brief ceremony."

Leigh smiled proudly. "I'll be ready, sir," she said.

She went straight to her and Kelly's office with the news. "Hey, Kelly," she said. "My commissioning paperwork came through. I want you to pin my bars on for me."

Kelly's eyes widened, and he jumped up and hugged her. "I would be proud to," he answered, "and congratulations."

He hugged her again, and they talked over their navy experiences over the last several years. They had worked together on everything.

While Kelly was very glad for Leigh, he knew he would miss being close to her. Fraternization rules would prevent them from ever hanging out together. They could work together professionally only.

"I won't handle this real well," Kelly finally said.

Leigh looked at him hard. "Yes you will," she said as she held both of his arms, "and we will work together as a team just like other officer and enlisted sailors do."

Leigh wished Bill could be here for this too. She had been gone from him for going on four months now.

She would have to e-mail back pictures. He would be so proud of her. Bill had encouraged her to try for the commission too, and now it was really going to happen!

Senior Chief Wilson and the YN1 set up the quarterdeck for the ceremony. They brought out the punch bowl and set out a small cake she had ordered from the DFAC.

Kelly went back to his can and put on his pressed desert uniform set, or DCUs. Leigh did the same.

When he walked in to rehearse the pinning, Kelly met with the senior chief to go over the details. As she recited the order and placement, Kelly struggled to put on his happy face.

"Ensign Select Andrews will come forward and stand here," she said. "You will come up and stand beside her. Captain Benton will hand you the gold ensign bars, and you will pin them on one at a time."

Kelly did his best to accept what was coming. Separation of personal association was fundamental to officer and enlisted performance. He had known about it for a long time and had forced himself to accept it. But now it hit him like a ton of bricks. His eyes widened, and he lost his composure for a few seconds.

Senior Chief Wilson touched him on the cheek. "Kelly, I'm here to talk after this is over. Everyone gets through it, even hard ones like this one's going to be."

Kelly started to cry and stopped himself. "Then I'll get through it too," he said. He turned and walked outside. Walking for a bit would help.

After lunch, Leigh went to her can to pack up her stuff. The berthing group had several sailors who had left for family and medical problems. They had an individual can to give her, like the other officers and chiefs had. They even helped bring her stuff over to her new location.

At 1400 hours (2 p.m.) the ceremony began. Leigh was the only one getting anything. There were no additional awards for other sailors. Captain Benton began by describing how it was an honor to commission one of his favorite petty officers.

"This is a very good part of my job as skipper," he said. "Ensign Select Andrews, would you come forward?"

Leigh stepped forward in her crisply pressed uniform. She had taken the MC1 patches off her desert uniform collar for this occasion.

"MC1 Raines, would you come forward for the pinning?"

Kelly stepped forward. He was very proud of Leigh and he wanted to show that pride. It was an honor for him to be asked to perform this task.

Captain Benton handed him the bright gold bars. As Kelly turned to pin them on, his eyes betrayed his inner emotions. Leigh was quick to catch on. Kelly swallowed hard, smiled, and pulled off the frog catches. He put one bar on her collar, opened the catches, and pushed them on. Then he did the other side. Kelly stepped back half a step, looked Leigh in the eye, and proudly saluted her. She returned her first salute as an officer, to her former best friend.

Kelly tried to stop his tears from falling, but no willpower in the world would help. It started Leigh's tears in response. Without even thinking, he did something that just wasn't done at a pinning ceremony. He bent forward and kissed Leigh on the cheek. Then he turned and walked back to the ranks of attending sailors.

No one moved for a long second. The emotion of the moment had stopped time for everyone. The senior chief, several women, and even some of the men were struck by the touching event.

Captain Benton stepped forward and reached out his hand to help break the tension. "Congratulations, Ensign Andrews. Let's give her a round of applause."

The ceremony attendees clapped loudly as the skipper turned Leigh around for all to see.

As soon as Captain Benton said at ease, Kelly slipped out the side door. He sobbed out loud for a few seconds. Then he walked back to his can alone.

No one realized Kelly had left, since he had tried to be as

discreet as possible. When Leigh realized he was gone, she started to go outside to look for him. Senior Chief Wilson stopped her.

"Not yet, Ensign," she said. "Stay here and let this be for a while."

Leigh didn't want to do what the senior chief said. But she grudgingly followed the experienced navy leader's insistence.

Later, Captain Benton came up to her. "Ensign, I want you to let Kelly be by himself this evening. I won't order or direct you to do that. But I want to ask you, let him get over this for now. It will work better this way. I'm asking you to trust me. Just talk with him again in the morning."

Leigh did what her commanding officer suggested. Later when she went to dinner, she didn't see Kelly at the DFAC at all.

After the meal, she walked to her new can. Leigh looked around at the four walls with no one to talk to and thought of her best navy friend.

But Kelly and Leigh wouldn't have time to worry about their emotions.

Senior Chief Wilson got the call for a press team at 0200 hours. The next morning, everyone was ushered into the conference room as soon as they reported to work. A convoy was going to Ramadi to meet with the local tribal leaders. Another two-star marine general would be the principal coalition force representative.

Meetings like this were kept unannounced for security reasons.

"I want MC1s Daniels and Raines to cover the meeting," said Wilson. "We need good shots of the handshakes and when they are sitting in the circle."

Arab tribal leaders commonly sat on the ground in a circle to discuss important issues. American officers were getting used to the custom.

At 0900 hours, the convoy stopped by the PAO building to pick up the MCs. The trip to Ramadi would take two hours. There were fifteen vehicles. Several Humvees had only drivers and A-drivers in an effort to confuse insurgents as to which vehicle held the general.

Gunners atop the equipped Humvees were especially cautious on this trip, and for good reason.

The convoy left and made good time. All went well until the convoy reached Ramadi. A Euphrates River town, sections of the town were in the flat bottomland river area and other parts were in the nearby rolling hills.

By late morning, the sun was shining brightly off the small gray and tan buildings that were common in the western Iraq Sunni religious area.

Just as the convoy pulled into the outskirts of the city, a huge IED went off. The fourth Humvee went straight up into the air. The fifth vehicle was disabled, and the door on one side was blown open. Insurgent gunshots rang out almost immediately toward the wrecked Humvees.

At once the American Humvee gunners answered back. The M240 Bravo machine guns from the first Humvees sprayed toward the enemy positions. In addition, shots from the even louder .50-caliber guns in the rear Humvees rang out.

Kelly and Daniels were in the eighth Humvee. They could see the occupants of the fifth Humvee firing back at the insurgents. But the occupants were taking more than they were able to give back. Kelly could hear screams of the wounded American soldiers.

Both sailors had already taken their weapons to condition one, with full magazines inserted and a live shell in the chamber. Kelly didn't think about it or tell Daniels what he was going to do. His camera came off, and the Humvee door just somehow flew open. Out he jumped and began running toward the closest disabled vehicle.

Halfway along his route, he saw five insurgents running in from a side street. They were firing toward the open Humvee. They hadn't seen Kelly coming from their left.

Kelly shoved his safety to full automatic and opened fire on the insurgents. Three of them dropped immediately. Two directed their fire back at Kelly.

He took a knee and tried to keep firing, but his magazine was empty. Kelly quickly grabbed another and shoved it in. He left the setting on full automatic.

The delay cost him. He took a round in his forward leg. But his second magazine proved deadly, and he dropped the remaining two insurgents.

He jumped up and ran for the Humvee. He could hear the cheers of the marines and sailors inside, who had seen the insurgents fall. Kelly's leg hurt, and he had to limp along. But his strength was still good, and he pulled the first soldier he came to out of the vehicle and carried him back to his Humvee. Kelly ran back for a second survivor. Rounds hit his vest as he headed back to the disabled Humvee. A stinging pain shot through his side as a round struck him through the open edge of his MTV vest.

The insurgents were trying to pick off Americans where their vests were vulnerable. Kelly could tell the bullet had not gone deep into anything. He picked up a second victim and carried him to a following Humvee. The occupants already had a door open.

Other Humvee occupants began to ignore protocol and helped carry the remaining wounded to various convoy vehicles.

It wasn't long before helicopters and a nearby army detachment came up to secure the scene.

"Here comes the cavalry," said Daniels.

The army squad's presence ended the battle. The remaining insurgents decided to retreat from the American firepower. The soldiers cleared a landing zone, and Medevac helicopters showed up to evacuate the wounded. Kelly was ordered to be among them. Saying he was fine didn't impress the convoy chain of command at all.

Kelly went straight to the triage hospital in Baghdad. He was kept in an emergency room ward while more seriously injured troops were treated first. When his turn came, the nurse immediately took off his boot and cut away his pant leg. The leg shot hadn't hit any bones and had passed straight through his calf muscle. The abdomen bullet had just gone through the skin and damaged a little bit of muscle in his side. Apparently the round had gone through the edge of his side and then hit the inside of his vest before falling down and away.

"The leg tendons and ligaments aren't damaged," said the attending doctor. "Your side will heal without stitches, but you'll be sore."

Kelly spent two days in the hospital there before being helicoptered back to Al Asad late the second day. When he landed, a military ambulance took him straight to the battalion aid station (BAS).

Leigh and Senior Chief Wilson were waiting. The army orderlies brought Kelly into his bed area. He was with several other soldiers wounded in previous battles.

"Hey there, guy," said Leigh as Kelly looked up. He put out his hand, and Leigh held it to her chest. Then she bent over and hugged Kelly. Her tears fell down onto him. The two sailors just stayed that way for a minute. Senior Chief Wilson put her hand on Kelly's shoulder, quietly crying herself.

The nurses brought Kelly a phone to call home. They stretched the cord to his bedside.

The home phone rang three times before Gwen picked up. She had just gotten up on her Friday off.

"Hello," she said.

"Hi, babe," said Kelly. "Been wounded a little bit but am going to be fine."

Gwen sucked the air out of the phone all the way back to Kansas. She couldn't speak for several seconds.

"Hey now, I said I'm all right," said Kelly.

Gwen finally spoke, mad at her husband for getting wounded, going to the war, and being in the navy altogether.

"How all right?" Gwen asked. She was immediately worried about IED casualties in which troops lost arms and legs. "Are you missing anything?" she fearfully asked.

"Everything is here," said Kelly. "I can get up and walk for my own head calls."

"Were you shot?" Gwen asked.

"Yes," Kelly said. "Once in the lower right leg and again in the right side. But I got five of them!"

Kelly went on to relay the battle story. Gwen could not have cared less if he was proud of his battlefield actions. She was mad at him, crying, and happy for his survival all at the same time.

Leigh went to see Kelly every day. Even if she was an officer, she was going. No one said anything to her. Since his wounds weren't severe, he would see a full recovery.

"I don't want to go home," he declared to the attending lieutenant colonel. "There is no reason to send me home."

"It's not up to me," said the army doctor. "But I will forward your request."

Not having any of his request was Senior Chief Wilson. "You are going home, Mr. Raines," she said. "I'm not going to lose a single member of our unit if I can help it."

Kelly respected his senior chief. But like Leigh, he didn't hold back when he had something he wanted to say. When the hospital released him to put weight on his leg and walk, he went straight to Captain Benton. Senior Chief Wilson saw him walk in, and for a moment they glared at each other.

"Skipper, there is no reason to send me home," he declared.

Captain Benton just sat there looking at him. "I don't like to override Senior Chief," he said. "She runs this place, if you haven't figured it out by now. I couldn't do this without her."

"We all know she does," said Kelly. "But even she can be wrong, and I want to stay."

Benton thought for a moment, before he spoke. "Kelly, I'll think about it."

Looking at the navy captain, Kelly didn't say anything for a few seconds. He got up, thanked the officer, and turned to leave.

"I really want to stay, sir," he said as he shut the door.

Kelly had to report to the BAS daily to have his leg checked. He had climbed into the helicopter without aid for his medevac trip from

Ramadi. Every day he had put weight on his leg. And now after three weeks, he was walking fine.

Leigh thought he should take his free offer to go home. "Gwen would slap you if she knew what you were saying," she said. "I may slap you."

"Well, get your hand ready," said Kelly.

Captain Benton met with the BAS doctors on a Monday morning and then went straight to his office. He called Senior Chief Wilson in and shut the door.

Kelly wanted to listen without being obvious. But when the voices became raised, he and everyone else nearby heard every word that was being said.

"You will never forgive yourself for not sending him home when you had the chance!" Wilson said, her voice carrying through the walls of the skipper's office.

Kelly's first thought questioned why he should be singled out to be sent back while Leigh and all the other sailors would be put in harm's way.

CHAPTER 9

Kelly was glad to have permission to stay. His leg wasn't really perfect, but he got around without a limp. He was allowed to go into the office and work.

He also got asked to assist with a suicide watch. A Seabee had been "Dear Johned" and was threatening to kill himself. Senior Chief Wilson asked Kelly to be on the watch team for Equipment Operator Second Class Jimmy Carr.

"We have been asked to take part of the schedule," Wilson said. "I want to send you until you are 100 percent ready to go outside the wire again. Remember, you can't take your gun."

Kelly took the afternoon watch and went to the can number for Carr. He knocked on the door and another Seabee opened it.

"Glad you're here," the watch stander said. "Are you my relief?"

"Yes," Kelly replied. "How's it going in there?"

The Seabee stepped outside and shut the door. He proceeded to give the pass-down instructions to Kelly.

"He's still in shock," the Seabee said. "But he's not over the edge. He just needs someone to be with him and listen, if he will ever talk."

"Well, I can do that," Kelly replied. "Go ahead and shove off."

Kelly went inside, said his name, and asked to shake hands with the EO. Carr shook his hand but just sat on his bed, holding a crumpled blue wrapped gift package.

Kelly spoke again. "Is there anything you want to talk about?" he asked.

"No," Carr said. He sat back on his bed, still holding the package.

The EO stayed that way until Kelly's relief came at suppertime. Carr didn't or wouldn't say a word.

At pass-down, Kelly asked his relief about the package.

"It was a belated Christmas present from his son," said the relief Seabee. "Some women are so cruel, to send a man divorce papers right at the holidays."

At the galley that night, Kelly went up to the table Leigh was sitting at. She was with a group of officers and chiefs.

"Hey, Ensign," he said.

"Hi, Kelly," replied Leigh. "How's the watch with the Seabee going?"

"Not good," he said. "Carr won't talk to me at all. He just sits there, not getting better."

"Are they going to ship him back stateside?" asked Leigh.

"I think so," Kelly said, "but we don't have any word on when that will be."

Kelly remembered some of his suicide prevention training lessons and decided to ask Leigh to help. "Ensign, would you come with me at my next watch? Carr won't open up to me, but he might if you came."

Leigh thought for a second before answering. "Let me run it by the chain of command," she said, "but I think I could come."

Kelly's next watch was the same time the following afternoon. Leigh got permission from the executive officer (XO) to assist.

Kelly came to get her shortly before their watch was to begin. She checked her weapon at the armory on the way.

The EO looked up with surprise as Leigh followed Kelly into the can.

"Petty Officer Carr, this is Ensign Andrews," Kelly said. "Would it be all right if she comes this afternoon?"

"I guess," Carr said.

Leigh shook his hand, sat on the other bed with Kelly, and let some time pass before she said anything. Finally, she asked Kelly if he would get her something to drink.

"Would you like something too?" she asked Carr.

"Okay," he replied.

Moving her lips soundlessly, she told Kelly to take his time coming back. Once he was gone, Leigh sat there for a minute before asking Carr if he wanted to talk. "I'm glad to just listen," she said.

The EO looked at her for a few seconds. Then he looked down and finally opened up. "My wife is divorcing me," he said. "She will take my little boy away. I should have left the 'Bees when they decided to deploy me."

Leigh didn't say a word. She was going to let Carr talk and get as much off his chest as possible.

"I didn't think things were all that bad," he said. "I don't want to live. I wish they would let me off myself." Carr paused for quite a while, so Leigh decided now was the time to say something.

"You don't want to do that," she said. "Your son would never get over your suicide, *ever*!" Leigh said, raising her voice.

The EO just looked down, not making eye contact.

"The navy will demobilize you soon," she said. "Would you consider some ideas from me?"

Carr didn't speak, so Leigh continued. "Sailors survive PTSD, POW situations, and amputations," she said. "They can survive Dear Johns, and you can too. There is a little boy who will want to see his dad. You can have that and much more to live for."

"I don't want to live if I can't be with Marquita," Carr said.

"Were you having trouble before you left?" Leigh asked.

"Yes," he said. "She was talking about divorce before I deployed."

"Well, your choice of staying with her has been taken away from you with the divorce papers," Leigh said. "When you do get home, you will have to go somewhere else. Do you have other family you could stay with for a while?"

"Yes," he answered. "I have an aunt who would be glad for me to come and stay and help her out."

"Let's do that then," Leigh said. "You will need to attend counseling as well. The navy will order it, whether we like it or not."

"I don't want to go," he said.

"Well, you can decide what you want to do when that time comes," Leigh answered. "Would you think on some ideas from me for now?"

"What are they?" he asked.

"Number one," Leigh said, "is being there for your little boy. Number two, would you ask some new women to go out with you? You could really do better than Marquita."

"I don't want to ask anybody out!" he insisted.

Leigh went on with what she wanted to say. "The world of dating is like a big lake. It is full of women to catch," she said. "Some men think they can't get a girl to like them back, and some men can get quite a few to like and want them."

Carr just sat there, but Leigh noticed he was listening and not shutting her out.

"Would you try something for me?" Leigh asked. "After you finish the counseling and you are at your aunt's home, would you ask ten girls to go out with you?"

"I haven't asked ten women my whole life!" Carr exclaimed.

"Like I said," she responded, "just ask ten. And don't let noes bother you. You get right back out there and ask the next woman to go out."

Leigh wanted to ask about his employment. "Do you have a job to go back to?"

"Yes," he said. "I drive a 'dozer for a pond building and terracing company. They don't pay that well. I think they will always have work for someone who knows how to push dirt."

"Just think on my ideas," Leigh said. "You have a good job, and you're a nice-looking man with a son. There are many single girls with kids too."

Leigh was in the process of going on when Kelly came back with the soft drinks.

"I want to give you my civilian business card," Leigh said. "It has my phone and e-mail contacts. Will you let me stay in contact with you?"

"Yes," the EO said.

Kelly could hardly believe the 100 percent turnaround he was seeing as Leigh continued.

"May I have your home contacts too?" she asked.

"Yes," Carr said. He went on to give them to her, and Leigh wrote them down in her wheel book.

Kelly, Leigh, and Carr drank cold sodas as they continued to visit. Leigh told Kelly that Carr's wife had filed for divorce and that he had a little boy. Kelly brought up the next point for the Seabee to consider.

"May I talk with you about your direct deposit pay?" he asked. "Is your pay being put into a joint account?"

"Yes, it is," Carr replied.

"Would you check to see how much is in there?" Kelly asked. "And if what I think has happened did, would you arrange to have your next check put into a new account?"

"I would need to go in the daytime," the Seabee said, now instinctively suspecting that his wife had cleaned him out.

"Let's go now," Kelly said. "Ensign has a vehicle, and we could ride with her."

The three went to the base computer lab, and Carr looked up his bank account. Kelly and Leigh stayed close. They suspected what he would discover.

"It's empty!" exclaimed Carr. "So is the savings account I had for my son!"

Kelly was quick to respond. "Then let's start the process to keep your next check from going there," he said. "We can do that at the combined forces bank."

Leigh drove the group to the bank, and they arranged to have Petty Officer Carr's money direct deposited into a new account at the military bank only.

Leigh said they had better work on the child support too. "You need to get the judge advocate corps to suggest a child support payment amount," she said. "Then you can arrange for it to be put into your old joint account or a separate one for your wife to get support for your son."

Leigh and Kelly took Carr to the JAG office. They weren't able to see a lawyer then, but they made an appointment to see one the next day. Then the group went back to Carr's can and stayed with him until their relief came. They included all that had happened in their pass-down for the following watch.

Kelly walked away with Leigh in total disbelief at how different this day had been from yesterday afternoon. "How on earth did you get him to open up like that?" he asked. "And look at what all we were able to do!"

"I just listened and asked to lend ideas," she replied. She related her dating ideas to him and told him how she had encouraged Carr to ask ten women out.

"You think he will do that?" Kelly asked.

"Nope," Leigh said, "but he might get to three. And I'm betting that one of them will say yes. God really does have someone for everyone, and he helps people if they will just ask."

Kelly and Leigh went on to talk about the Seabee, home life, and the strange things they had ended up doing for the navy.

At supper, they sat together with other officers and enlisted sailors. Kelly was glad to get to talk to his best friend again. He guessed he had found a way to get around fraternization rules.

Leigh was a very special girl in Kelly's eyes. He wondered if Bill knew how lucky he was.

The next day at his watch, Kelly took Carr to see the JAG lawyer. Carr got help setting up his child support and additional advice on how to coordinate his divorce with the JAG office in Gulfport, Mississippi, where he would demobilize.

Leigh came to help him with divorce details several times over the next week.

"You have to follow what your attorney will want for you to do," she said. "He's the boss."

Carr didn't want to pay additional legal fees.

"You know, she left me," he said. "Shouldn't that make her the 'at fault' party?"

"Forget fault," Leigh said. "You want to put obtaining shared custody of your son first and foremost. That is how you get to be with him. It also gets you out of providing all of the support, which she and her lawyer will try hard for."

Carr worried that his continued enlistment would make him a possibility for another call-up. "Won't she get favored by the judge for me being a Seabee?" Carr asked.

Leigh knew plenty of sailors who had joint custody.

"The judge will respect your service," she said. "It's the suicidal thoughts we want out of court."

Carr opened his eyes wide as he realized that. "I wish I had gotten counseling help when I found out Marquita left me," he said.

"Well," Leigh said, "you have it now. Let's go into court and see if you can get through the hearings without that coming out. Marquita doesn't know about it yet, and we certainly aren't going to tell her."

Carr was like many suicidal people; they really could change their minds with the right help. That was what the navy was providing for him, from Kelly and especially through Leigh.

The Seabee chain of command noticed the improvement in Carr's mental state. Their skipper personally thanked Kelly and Leigh for their help. But they didn't change their minds about demobilization. Petty Officer Carr was still going home.

Kelly and Leigh went to see him as he waited for his ride to the AACG-DACG.

"Be sure to file for divorce when you see the JAG attorney back in Gulfport," Leigh said.

"I will," Carr said. "I will call my son too and tell him I'm coming home."

Leigh and Kelly thought Petty Officer Carr had a real chance of making it. But only time would tell if he would be able to stand the stress of the legal action, home life changes, and civilian employer stress.

"I think he will make it," Leigh said to Kelly.

"I think he will too," Kelly answered. "He has to want to, and now I think he does."

Chapter 10

Leigh was not happy that she had been prevented from going on the Ramadi convoy. She had requested to be sent on the next mission when it came in.

The COP in Anah was almost complete. Benton needed a story for *Naval Reservist Magazine*. Ensign Andrews was familiar with the personnel there and argued her case to the skipper.

"MC1 Daniels could work under me," she said to Benton. "Petty Officer Raines could go on the next convoy, if he is 100 percent by that time."

The captain made the decision to send her. He directed Senior Chief Wilson to notify the sailors and coordinate for the trip.

Kelly was not happy about it at all. He was at the BAS when Leigh made her case to the skipper. He already knew about the press assignment. He just wasn't told who was going until he walked back into the office. The Seabee convoy was already loading at the PAO building.

Leigh was getting ready to go at her new desk in the officers' room. It was just down the passageway from where she and Kelly had sat. He invited himself into the officers' room.

"You don't need to go," he said. "MC1 Daniels can handle this by himself."

Leigh puffed up at hearing his opinion. "I'm going, MC1," she said, using his military rank. She did that when she wanted him to forget that she was a woman or needed protection.

Kelly knew when she wanted him to shut up. But like her, if

he had something to say, especially concerning her, he didn't care if she or anyone else liked it.

"That place is a death trap. This story is not more important than you."

Leigh ignored him and picked up her MTV vest and helmet. She could have used him to help her put in on, but she wasn't about to ask now. Leigh gave a big heave and hoisted the vest over her head.

"I don't want you to go," said Kelly. He was crying now.

Leigh knew better than to look at him. She grabbed her M16 and hurried out the door to meet the convoy.

I didn't train for this to come here and type in the office, she thought. *I can shoot a gun too.*

It was late afternoon when the convoy started out. There were six total vehicles—four Humvees and two flatbed trucks. Two Humvees had M240 Bravo machine guns mounted.

The convoy would be taking building materials out for the Seabees as well as bringing back equipment from the almost-complete project. Leigh would stay there only through the following day and come back that evening. Because of the recent increase in insurgent IED attacks, the risk was high, or red, now on all the roads leading to the new COP.

The drive out didn't take as long as last time, as the roundabout routes were now just as dangerous as the shorter ones. They made it in just over two hours, without any explosions or insurgent small arms fire.

Leigh and MC1 Daniels ate a late evening MRE supper before spending the night in the new SWA hut barracks completed by the Seabees. They went to work on the story first thing the next morning.

"Let me shoot, ma'am," said Daniels. "You're familiar with all of the people, and I can just follow you."

"Sounds good, MC1. I'll get my notepad."

Leigh and Petty Officer Daniels walked all over the COP. The marine barracks they stayed in were exceptionally nice. Daniels got good pictures of the sandbags in the roof above the bed areas. The design would help protect the sleeping marines from indirect fire at night from enemy mortar and rocket attacks.

Next they took photos and wrote notes about the small DFAQ, base chapel, and office quarters. Then, with their story quotes and photography all done, Leigh and Daniels ate a late MRE lunch and waited for the convoy to leave. Under new orders to leave early, they headed out just before 1400 hours. In order to change their route, they would be going on a little-used road through the small town of Hodah.

All was quiet as the convoy came into the edge of town. Small tan and gray buildings with dusty windows and flat roofs were all the troops could see. The only paved road was the one they were on, and they approached a market area similar to a town square.

At the center of town, beside the market and what looked like a government building, the insurgents struck. With small arms and RPGs, they shot at the convoy. The M240 Bravo machine guns on the Humvees answered back immediately. The firefight quickly became hot. The convoy didn't stop.

Then they hit the IED. Leigh's Humvee went up on its side from the explosion. The hastily placed IED and subsequent blast hadn't made a direct hit. Her ears rang loudly, even with her earplugs in. She couldn't see anything.

Leigh was scared to death, but she wasn't hiding. As her professional training and instincts kicked in, she immediately went to condition one with the M16 she had held onto during the blast. She and Daniels unbelted and crawled down into the rear corner of the Humvee. The front and rear windows were all they could see out of.

The driver and A-driver were in the process of unbelting as well when the insurgents directed their fire at the front of the Humvee. Then an RPG found its target. In a blinding flash of light, the grill of Leigh and Daniel's Humvee was hit. The driver and A-driver were both seriously hurt and burned by the blast.

Again, Leigh could hardly hear because of the extremely loud concussion blast. Being in the back and behind two rows of seats kept Leigh and Daniels from the worst of the explosion.

With overwhelming force, the M240 Bravo machine guns in the nearby Humvees answered back in the direction of the RPG fire. The trail from the shoulder fired rocket shell told the American gunners exactly where to shoot.

Soon the terrorist fighters backed away from the horrendous pounding and fled through the town. When the all clear was ordered, the nearby vehicles emptied and the troops ran toward Leigh's Humvee. She and Daniels were already trying to help the drivers.

Leigh had crawled past the front seat console area, where she checked the wounds of both equipment operators. They were conscious but badly burned. She helped the personnel outside the vehicles lift the men out through the one door they could access. Daniels helped push them up to the marines, sailors, and Seabees outside.

The master chief radioed for a helicopter to take the wounded. It looked like both drivers would survive their burns, if they could get to the BAS in time. The pilot would take them straight to Baghdad.

Leigh and MC1 Daniels crowded into another Humvee and headed out after the scene was secured. The wounded were taken in the helicopter.

Kelly had come back into the PAO office after supper. He wanted to be there to hear any news about the convoy. He knew they would be coming back that evening.

Senior Chief Wilson got the message from the duty officer earlier, that the convoy had been hit. She walked into the lobby area and told the sailors there what had happened, including Kelly. His heart hit the deck.

"Which Humvee was hit?" asked Kelly.

"It was the one Leigh was riding in," said Wilson. "We don't know who was hurt yet. They don't say personnel over the radio or telephone."

Kelly was overcome with anxiety at her words. All they could do now was wait.

"They will be back in less than two hours. We'll know something then."

The two-hour wait seemed like two years. Kelly and Senior Chief Wilson found themselves pacing the floor. Wilson got word that the convoy was going straight to the Seabee compound.

"I want to go to the Seabee Camp," said Kelly.

"I'm going with the skipper," said Wilson. "I'll ask him if you can come too."

When it was finally time to load up, the three sailors got into the PAO van. The captain had agreed to let MC1 Raines go. They would hopefully be picking up Leigh and MC1 Daniels. It was starting to get dark as they pulled into the compound to wait for the convoy.

Many of the Seabees were at the ECP, waiting to hear about their shipmates. Nervous chiefs and officers stood. Since they had been through this many times now, they weren't openly emotional. They were past that. They just stood, unable to sit because of the tension.

As the lights from the convoy came into sight, everyone stood alongside the entrance.

The convoy pulled through the gate and didn't stop until the vehicles were at the back lot. Then everyone piled out. Kelly and his PAO group had walked beside the vehicle they hoped their shipmates were in.

As the doors opened, Kelly noticed there was no one inside whom he knew. His breathing stopped. Then he looked behind him and saw Leigh and Daniels climbing out of another Humvee. He ran to them.

Kelly sobbed out loud upon seeing Leigh, and he hugged her tightly. She was covered in dirt, dark dust, and what looked like blood spatter.

"I'm all right, Kelly," she said. "You can let go of me now."

Kelly didn't let go. The group walked back to the van and headed back to the PAO complex.

At the office, the skipper and senior chief helped Leigh and MC1 Daniels bring their gear inside. Even though it was against protocol, the PAO sailors all kept their MTV vests at their workplace.

They sat down at the picnic table that served as the board table in the meeting room.

"Kelly, I think Ensign Andrews is going to live," said Senior Chief Wilson. "You haven't let go of her since she got out of the Humvee!"

It was very improper for enlisted sailors to do this with officers. No one had said anything because of their respect for Kelly and Leigh. But it was starting to become awkward. Leigh finally grabbed Kelly's arm and got up.

"Let's go," she said, trying to remove the problem from the room. "Walk me back to my can."

The back passageway was the closest exit to the cans. Most of the enlisted sailors used this door when they came to and from work. The officers shared SUVs and typically used the front door. The skipper's stateroom was at the office, along with senior chiefs. They didn't use this door like the enlisted did.

Leigh and Kelly hadn't made it very far down the back passageway when Kelly stopped Leigh and pulled her into the storeroom, where the PAO sailors kept their camera and video equipment.

"Why did you go?" sobbed Kelly aloud as he pulled Leigh so tightly to him that she could feel his heartbeat. "Why did you go?" he said once more.

Leigh didn't think before she did what came next. She raised her chin, looked at him for long second, and then kissed him on the lips.

Kelly's eyes widened. He didn't think either as he paused for a brief second and then kissed her right back.

Then Kelly and Leigh crossed the line between close friends and lovers. Like other affairs between good people, the participants don't plan them. They don't know how they happen. They just do.

Kelly didn't know how he got enough of his and her clothing off to make love. She didn't know or remember either. They just found themselves past the point of no return. Doing what spontaneous lovers do, they did the whole thing against the wall in the back of a storage room in Iraq.

The fact that it was war didn't make it right or justify anything. The Bible both Leigh and Kelly read stated that the seventh commandment—adultery—is wrong. The scriptures emphasize that God will help people resist any and all temptations, if Christians will just ask.

Well, that was all fine and good, but Kelly and Leigh were as they were. His big arms bulged as he held Leigh off the deck, making love loudly against the storage room bulkhead.

CHAPTER 11

The next morning, Kelly and Leigh found themselves inside an abandoned base building near the PAO office. Somehow they had come up with a few tarps and had used them for bedding.

Kelly didn't know how many times they had made love. Both of them had almost completely walled out their homes, families, and religious convictions. Until morning, anyway.

It was a Saturday. That meant another typical workday in the war.

"What are we going to do now?" asked Kelly.

"*Shh*," said Leigh. "We're going to go to work just like always. Now let go of me."

Kelly had held her all night. But it wasn't just him; she had also given in to what had happened. She was just as responsible as he was.

They got up and dressed. Their booty call quarters hadn't been much. Leigh did her best to fluff out her sex hair, before they walked out the door.

"Do you want to walk back separately?" Kelly asked.

Leigh ignored him. Kelly's roommate had probably figured out what happened. The senior chief was too experienced not to see it. Right now, Leigh just wanted to get to her can and clean up. Her uniform still had blood on it from the RPG attack.

Kelly and Leigh made it back to their cans and hit the showers.

At work, the senior chief immediately directed Leigh to go back to her can. Sailors who had been in IED attacks were required to take immediate downtime. Because severe traumatic situations were horrific, participants typically needed time to accept what they'd been through. Taking time to think about family and what had just happened could help sailors accept what took place and deal with it objectively so that they could better and more properly return to duty.

Not being able to sleep greatly affects a person's ability to cope. In this case, that wasn't the problem with Leigh. Kelly stayed at the office all morning. No one said anything to him about the previous night.

At noon, Leigh heard a soft knock on her door. She opened it quickly, knowing that it would be Kelly.

"Get in," she said.

They picked up where they had left off earlier that morning. After about forty-five minutes, conscious thought set in.

"This has to end sometime," Leigh said as Kelly got ready to go back to the office.

"I know," he said. "But I just want you."

"It needs to be soon, Kelly," she said. "We both know it!"

Kelly nodded and ducked out the door.

That night after supper, Leigh looked to see if Kelly was waiting for her outside the DFAC. They hadn't said anything to each other about it. She felt he would know to meet her, and he did.

Kelly was standing just past the weapon clearing barrels. She walked to him, and they headed back to their abandoned building. Somehow, two pillows and several blankets had made their way to the building. Leigh saw them, smiled, and looked at Kelly with a "how did you do that" expression.

"Don't ask," he said.

Leigh and Kelly spent their second night together. He held her just as tightly as the night before. Leigh pulled him toward her just the same.

Before people have affairs, they fall in love. Kelly and Leigh had done that, though they didn't realize it, well before they went to war.

People meet others they like, and almost everyone is strong enough to resist. They are adult enough to do what is right. The problem is when two people like each other back. That's when it gets tough, and that was what happened to Leigh and Kelly.

If they had stayed stateside, the affair would never have happened. But the IED attacks increased the stress, past the point where they could resist their temptations.

They were, however, strong enough to begin to say no, Leigh more so than Kelly. And that was about to happen.

Sunday morning rolled around quickly. Kelly and Leigh were regulars at church services. But they didn't go today. They stayed together at their building, instinctively knowing that their time together as lovers was about to end.

By late morning, Kelly spoke. Leigh had been trying to get up the courage to say what needed to be said.

"We better get something to eat before work," he said. On Sundays, everyone had to report by one in the afternoon.

"I know," said Leigh. "Kelly, it's about time."

He turned around and held her for a long second. Tears streamed from both eyes. "Not yet," he said. "No."

Like most men, Kelly wasn't as emotionally strong as Leigh.

"Let me think about it," said Leigh. By the sound of her words, Kelly didn't know if she would come to him again. And if she did, it would definitely be the last time.

They went to the DFAC and sat together this time. If anyone noticed, nothing was said. Officers and enlisted members sat together much of the time anyway.

At work that afternoon, Senior Chief Wilson and Executive Officer Jones called both Leigh and Kelly into the senior chief's office. Captain Benton allowed her to take the lead over the executive officer in this instance. There was no complaint from LCDR Jones.

Page thirteens were the punitive documents the navy used for sailor discipline, and none lay on the senior chief's desk. There was no talk of going to captain's mast, the highest form of discipline short of a court martial. She and the XO called the two in and shut the door. Kelly and Leigh knew their senior chief well enough, to know they were about to get it big time.

"It needs to stop," she said loudly. "I mean now!" Wilson glared at both of her sailors.

Kelly didn't say anything. Leigh cried quietly. Senior Chief Wilson paused for several seconds to let her words sink in. Then she spoke.

Going over military law, Wilson discussed the punishments for officer-enlisted fraternization violations, military codes of ethics, and both sailors' families back home. LCDR Jones never said a word.

She didn't grill the two with extensive questions. She just demanded an immediate end to the affair. Both sailors agreed.

"Kelly," said Wilson. "You're going out on a convoy tomorrow to the new forward operating base at Al-Quim."

Jones spoke next. "Ensign, you're still staying in for a few more days. Not because of the affair. Just standard procedure following an attack. You can work at your desk this afternoon."

Senior Chief Wilson looked at the XO, prompting him to briefly speak and end the disciplinary meeting with the typical order.

"Everything Senior has said is the way it is," the XO insisted, "from the skipper on down. You are dismissed."

As the workday ended at 1800, Kelly found himself still looking in Leigh's direction. He knew the directive from the senior chief and XO was the same thing as a direct order. But Kelly couldn't help himself. As is the case with many affairs, emotional attachments had formed. All he wanted to do was see Leigh again, enough so that he would disobey a direct order.

But Kelly wasn't the only one doing the thinking. Leigh wasn't able to work all afternoon. All she could think about was the affair, her marriage vows, and her husband, Bill. She also thought of seeing Kelly one more time and spending another night together.

But Leigh had a little more willpower. Whether it was because she was a woman or just able to see right and wrong, she knew she had to end this. Even if Kelly wasn't emotionally strong enough, she was.

At the end of the day, Leigh got up from her desk and left without speaking to Kelly. At the galley, she sat with the other officers. Kelly sat by himself.

She saw him get up to leave first. Leigh knew he would be waiting outside the DFAC by the weapon clearing station, the same place as the night before.

When Leigh got up later to walk out the exit door with the other women officers, she looked up and met Kelly's eyes. They looked at each other like people having affairs do.

Then Leigh swallowed hard, turned, and walked away toward the cans.

She began to cry and then softly sob. Some of the women officers tried to put their arms around her. But after a long second, she shrugged them off. Leigh ran ahead for a few lengths and then walked quickly back to her can and shut the door.

Kelly watched the whole thing, his heart hurting just as badly. He knew she was right. The senior chief was right. But he still walked back to the abandoned building.

The blankets and pillows were still there. He began to cry. Kelly looked at the room for several seconds. He brought one of the pillows up to his face. He could still smell Leigh's hair and lotion.

Kelly paused for a minute. As his free-flowing tears stained the pillow, he remembered their two nights together. Then he pulled the door shut and walked back to his can.

At first his thoughts were only of Leigh. Then he began to go back to Gwen, where he should have been. She had never had an affair on him.

This was my first and last, he said to himself.

Kelly spent the rest of his sleepless night drifting between thoughts of Leigh and thoughts of his wife, who had been good to him in every way.

Kelly had suffered from a very bad reaction to the flu a year before. He had been sick in bed for three weeks and had lost a tremendous amount of weight.

Gwen took care of me through all of that, he thought. He needed to get Leigh out of his mind and heart and continue to dwell on the Kansas farm girl who had given him all her devotion.

Back at her can, Leigh tossed, turned, and cried herself to sleep, at times sobbing for several minutes. Like Kelly, Leigh too was trying to move past her affair and back to the marriage she belonged to. Bill was just as devoted to her.

She knew Kelly would be getting up at 0400 to get ready for the convoy. If it was any other trip, she would certainly not have gone to see him off. But this was a highly dangerous trip. The convoy would probably struggle through one or more IEDs.

"I'm going," she said to herself. "But just to support my shipmate. The affair is over!"

CHAPTER 12

Kelly was up before his alarm went off. He tried not to wake his roommate. He dressed by flashlight, tucked his shaving kit into his already packed seabag, and placed it on his back like a backpack.

He got on his bicycle, flipped his lights on, and pedaled to the PAO office. He hadn't been there very long when Leigh showed up in the duty vehicle. Without even thinking about it, tears rolled down his cheeks as he looked at her. She walked up and hugged him.

Other sailors were there already. Senior Chief Wilson came in but didn't say a word to Leigh, for being there or even look at her hard.

The Seabee convoy would stop by the PAO office to pick Kelly up. Just a few minutes later they rolled up, their lights shining brightly.

The senior chief and Leigh helped Kelly carry his equipment and walked beside him to the Humvee he was to ride in. He hoisted on his MTV vest, and Leigh helped him adjust it. They set his gear inside the vehicle, and Kelly turned to say good-bye.

"We're not going to kiss," she assertively whispered.

"I know," he replied.

Kelly reached out and hugged her hard. Leigh hugged him right back. Then Kelly looked into her eyes. There was no stopping the brief kiss. It was stronger than any willpower. Even though it lasted only for the briefest second, it felt like an eon for Kelly and Leigh.

Leigh turned and walked back to where Wilson was standing.

The senior chief didn't say a word, even though big tears rolled down Leigh's cheeks as she quietly cried.

Wilson made a habit of sitting by the radio when her people left on convoys. She would stay there until Kelly was all the way to the FOB. This time, Leigh stayed at the office too. Usually she would walk back to the DFAC for breakfast if she came in this early. But not today.

It was not a typical road trip for the convoy. All the riders were very alert because the risk for IED attack was so high.

Kelly looked out the Humvee window as the dimly lit Seabee convoy came toward the top of a hill. The sky had an eerie darkness, as the cloud cover let only a portion of the morning light shine onto the roadway ahead.

All the sailors knew how dangerous it was to ride in the convoys and how high the risk of IED attack was. But no one was shaking in his or her boots. There were no late prayers, no upset stomachs, and no one wanted to go back home to Mommy.

Kelly wasn't afraid to die. Like Leigh, his senior chief, and his skipper, he would give his life for his country if he had to. There was no backing down from that commitment, that sense of duty.

No school really teaches troops to be that way. They really don't know where it comes from. It's just there, instinctively. It's similar to the way parents protect their children and the way men throw themselves in front of women during shootings. It's the way people dying of lingering illnesses stoically relax, say their good-byes, shut their eyes, and pass away.

Kelly thought about home, Gwen, and her farm. *I am going to dedicate myself to her and our life together,* he said to himself. *Leigh isn't leaving Bill, and I'm certainly not leaving Gwen. This is what God wants me to do, and what I want to do.*

Those were the last words Kelly thought. As the convoy came down the hill to cross the culvert of the dry creek bed, a flash of light went off. Kelly and the other Humvee occupants didn't hear or feel the massive explosion.

Leigh was in her office when she heard Senior Chief Wilson scream. She ran toward her open door. Her face was shaking with fright as she came up to Wilson's desk. The two women looked at each other for a second. Then the sound of the radio crackled.

"All clear," said the voice. "Get out of your vehicles and approach the downed Humvees."

Wilson finally spoke first. "I don't know which ones are hit," she said emotionally. "This time they didn't say the vehicle number."

Leigh and Wilson stood in her office for several minutes praying for good news. After a while they began to walk the passageways, anything to work off the stress.

Captain Benton had rushed over from his stateroom, after Senior Chief Wilson sent word to him.

"If anyone's hurt, we will get the news this morning," he said. "Stay here if you want to. When I know, you will know."

More people came into the office, and the silence was deafening. The radio talked about several Humvees being hit by the IED. The Seabee convoy was ordered back to the base, canceling the trip to the FOB. A commanding voice ordered all radio traffic to go to secure communications only.

About forty-five minutes later, Senior Chief Wilson saw the Seabee skipper come in. He went straight to Benton's office.

Wilson and Leigh came onto the quarterdeck area. Benton didn't talk with the Seabee commander very long. He stepped out of his office, looked right at the senior chief and Leigh, and then spoke.

"Kelly died in the explosion," he said. "He and the other occupants were dead when the corpsmen and Seabees pulled them out of the Humvee."

Wilson and Leigh just stood there for a few seconds, their eyes wide with shock. Leigh put her hands to her face, and Wilson immediately hugged her. Benton walked over and did the same thing. Other sailors joined in the group hug.

That was the scene inside the public affairs office, and it was the military way when someone gave his or her life for their country.

Leigh became inconsolable. Wilson and Benton had to walk

her into the skipper's office. Other people arriving got the news and added to the grief already present.

Benton asked the Seabee skipper to make sure river city had been initiated for the base. This was an immediate shutdown of personnel communication from the front line. The Seabee commander walked around to the offices and assisted the petty officers with securing their computer systems and ordering that no one e-mail or telephone home until after river city was lifted.

This was a good thing. It kept military friends from beating the system to the proper notification procedures.

It was late morning before Leigh was fit to leave the PAO building. Senior Chief Wilson refused to let her go by herself. She directed Lieutenant Junior Grade Hinton to stay with her at all times. Wilson drove them back to Leigh's can.

"Don't let her leave," said Wilson, "and come get me if anything goes wrong."

Military groups weren't really set up for grief-stricken situations. And a small two-person bunkroom wasn't the best place to recover from loss.

Leigh sat on her bed for maybe ten minutes. Then she got up and headed for the door.

"Hold on there," said the JG. "Let's stay right here."

"I'm leaving," said Leigh. "You can come or not."

Hinton accompanied Leigh with no idea where she was going. Leigh walked straight to the abandoned building where she and Kelly had gone for their two nights together. The pillows and blankets were still there. Leigh took one look and began to sob uncontrollably again. She picked up a pillow and held it tightly.

The J. G. didn't know what to say. Coming to see this wasn't what she had wanted to do, but she stayed with Leigh in spite of her personal thoughts.

Leigh asked her to go get a trash bag. After making sure Leigh was going to stay there, Hinton ran back to her can and got two large black bags from the roll.

She returned to find that Leigh had folded up the blankets.

She put everything into both bags, and they carried them back to Leigh's can.

Leigh put both bags on the side of her room.

The J. G. didn't say anything. She helped Leigh make room for them and then sat with her the rest of the day.

The next day, Leigh told Hinton that she wanted to call on Senior Chief Wilson. Her normal route would have been through the XO now that she was an officer, but the XO was on his way to central command in Baghdad, tending to PAO duties for the skipper. Benton had asked his senior chief to take over some of the XO duties in his absence.

The J. G. walked with Leigh back to the PAO building. Then they separated, with Hinton going to her desk and Leigh going straight to Wilson's office.

"How's it going?" asked the senior chief.

"I want to go to Kelly's funeral," Leigh said. "I want to apply for emergency leave."

Wilson just sat at her desk as Leigh made her request. Then she got up and closed the door. She didn't wait to hear the ensign say any more about it.

"Leigh, you're not going. The answer is no."

"I want to go," said Leigh. "I can apply for this, and you and the skipper have the ability to approve it. I want you to say yes."

"Leigh, there is something you don't know. Just listen for a minute. When you came back from your near-miss IED explosion, you and Kelly went to the back room here at the office. We heard you making love, slamming into the bulkhead—the skipper, MC1 Daniels, and me. We knew about your affair from the beginning!"

Leigh's eyes opened wide, and she felt great embarrassment as she remembered. She put her hands to her reddening cheeks and felt the heat. She didn't know they had heard.

Wilson continued, "You've had an affair with an enlisted man, against all fraternization policies. You are not going to Kelly's funeral. Even if you hadn't had the affair, the request would have been denied. You can go see his family when your deployment is over, but I don't think you should."

Leigh sat for a few seconds. "I don't care," she said. "I loved that man. I'm going to turn in the request anyway. Oh—" She began to sob uncontrollably again.

Wilson got up, sat in the chair next to Leigh, and put her hand on Leigh's shoulder. She didn't say anything, just sat there, expressing her care and concern for her shipmate and friend.

Leigh got up and didn't say a word. She opened the office door and walked out. Hinton was standing near the quarterdeck. As Leigh headed out the front door, Hinton looked at Wilson, shrugged, and followed Leigh outside to her quarters.

Leigh went back the next day and picked up the emergency leave application. She even filled it out, but she never turned it in.

She desperately wanted to go, for Kelly. No one there would know about the affair. But she did know that her leadership cared about her deeply. This was how they thought she should handle it. Maybe they were right.

CHAPTER 13

Gwen's sister Jane had been up about an hour. Her husband, David, had just left for work. Besides being the minister at Sherwin Christian Church, he worked at a funeral home during the week.

She had just loaded the washing machine and turned it on when the phone rang.

"Hello," said Jane as she wondered who it was. The caller ID showed US government.

"Is this Jane Griffin?" asked the caller.

"Yes," said Jane.

"This is Lieutenant Commander Russell from the naval reserve center in Kansas City. You are listed to call on Petty Officer Raines's notification list."

Jane's breath caught, and she tried to concentrate as her stomach knotted tightly. Her subconscious instincts told her what had happened.

"I regret to inform you of the death of Petty Officer Raines in Iraq. He asked for you to be a part of the spousal notification party."

Oh no, Jane thought and struggled to stay focused. "Yes, I want to be there when whoever comes to tell Gwen."

"It's us, and we're leaving in a few minutes," said the lieutenant commander. "I have your husband listed as the minister. Can you get him on a cell phone?"

"Yes, he just left. I can catch him before he gets to work."

"Is there a central location where we could meet?"

"Yes," said Jane. "Gwen's office is in Joplin on Range Line. If we met at the Petro Truck stop on I-44 just west of the Highway 71 interchange, we could drive together from there."

"I and one of my petty officers will leave shortly. MapQuest shows the drive will take two hours and fifteen minutes. Will that work for you?"

"That would be fine," said Jane. "Now, when should we meet you there?"

"It's 8:20 here," said the lieutenant commander. "Would 10:45 work?"

"Yes," Jane said. "I can turn David around and have him come get me." Then she asked, "How did Kelly die?"

"We don't have that information yet," said the lieutenant commander. "But when more is released, I would be glad to go over the details with you."

Both callers exchanged cell phone numbers, and Jane got ahold of David.

Gwen went to work on a typical day at the office. It was a bright midwestern morning as she drove into the sun toward the orthodontist office. She adjusted her visor to help block the glare.

Living west of town in Kansas made her drive east toward Joplin. She had the sun in her eyes going to work, and in the winter she had the sun in her eyes going home.

The office was unusually busy for a Monday morning. They had brackets to adjust, lost retainers to remold, and the usual emergencies. By late morning, the office had already seen 20 patients.

Brandi, the receptionist, looked up and saw the uniformed navy men walking through the front door. She also noticed a very distraught couple following behind them. As they came in through the double doors, the brilliant gold on the officer's dark blue uniform caught her eye. Then she saw the tears streaming down the faces of the couple.

A horrible feeling came over her as she realized what was going on. Kelly was the only navy husband in Iraq. She couldn't breathe and tried to speak but couldn't get anything to come out.

Lieutenant Commander Russell stepped up to the counter. "Ma'am," he said. "I need you to get ahold of yourself, so I can notify Mrs. Raines."

Brandi swallowed hard, but she couldn't make herself stop shaking. The office manager stepped out of her office, having heard and seen everything.

"Wait right there," she said. "I'll go get Gwen."

Naomi had been office manager for twelve years and she had handled some things similar to this before, but never this bad. She walked into the patient room where Gwen was assisting the orthodontist. Professional as Naomi was, she couldn't hide her face. She walked up and held Gwen's arm.

"Gwen," she said, "just hold on and walk with me to the front."

"What's wrong?" asked the mystified Gwen.

The two women stepped out of the patient room and walked along the passageway toward the front area. Gwen saw the navy uniforms first. Then she saw Jane and David. Tears were streaming down David's face.

Then it hit her like an emotional ton of bricks. Gwen's eyes opened wide as she realized what was happening, and her scream shuddered the entire office.

The reserve center skipper never got to say a word. Gwen ran around the navy sailors and straight to the grieving embrace of Jane and David.

Josh looked up from the maintenance he and his fellow firemen were performing on a truck in the open bay. He wondered what the naval officer and his own chaplain were doing here.

The chaplain pointed out which fireman was Joshua.

"Joshua Raines?" asked the officer.

"Yes," said Josh as he walked over to the men. He still didn't realize what had happened.

"I regret to inform you of the death of your father in Iraq. I received the notification this morning, and Chaplain O'Brian and I want to be here for you during this time."

Josh's eyes widened, and he couldn't speak for moment. Like

many young men who had not experienced sudden death, he didn't emotionally accept all that had just taken place or was about to take place.

"How did he die?" asked Josh.

"He was killed in action," said the lieutenant. "That's all the information I have. But as soon as I get more details, I will pass them on to you."

Josh began to cry, and as he did, the firefighters in the station house came and put their arms around him. It was their way, as when they lost a man in a fire. Word was passed around the firehouse, soon there were twenty firefighters joining in the group hug.

Chaplain O'Brian said he could take over from there. The navy XO nodded at his relief, and went back to the Kansas City Reserve Center.

Jane and David stayed with Gwen all night. She was inconsolable. When she tried to sleep, she would startle awake and bawl aloud. Jane found herself wishing she wasn't there.

It was almost like when someone was dying of a lingering illness, where death would bring silence, peace and be a blessing.

Jane finally got into bed with Gwen and tried that. They had slept together as little girls, and after most of the night going so badly, Jane didn't care how unusual it might appear. It helped. Gwen finally stayed asleep for two hours, and Jane got some much needed rest.

David got up from his bed on the too short couch, and showered in Gwen's bathroom. He found one of Kelly's razors and shaved. Then he woke Jane.

"Jane," he said softly, trying not to wake Gwen and have to listen to her sobs again.

Jane rolled a red eye open and looked at him.

"I really can't miss work today if I can help it," he said.

"I know," said Jane. "Be quiet with the door so you don't wake her up. We'll be fine, I think."

David nodded and quietly closed both the bedroom and then the front doors of Gwen's house.

Gwen stayed in bed all day. Visitors came by throughout the morning and afternoon. Jane had to tell them that Gwen wasn't able to see anybody. They all expressed their condolences and wished Gwen the best.

Food was stacked up all over the kitchen and hallway. The fridge was full, so she started putting it in the living room.

I don't know how we will have enough people to eat all of this, Jane thought.

Gwen's daughter had come the evening before and was there this evening too. She sat on the couch beside Jane.

"If she gets up, I want to be here," Laura said to Jane. "In case she wants to talk. I'm worried Mom won't get over this for a while."

At about a quarter to eight, Gwen got up to go to the bathroom. She saw Laura sitting in the living room. As Laura stood up, Gwen walked over to her and started bawling again. Laura held her mom for several seconds before Gwen finally said she had to pee.

Hoping Gwen would come back into the living room to talk, Laura sat down on the couch. Jane said that was a good idea, and she moved into the rocking chair.

As Gwen walked back down the hallway, she started to go back into the bedroom but stopped herself. She came in and sat down by Laura.

Laura had never seen her mom look so bad. It was like she had come down with the flu. Her face was pale, and both eyes were swollen.

Laura held Gwen's hand and didn't complain when her mom started to cry again. No one really talked; they just stayed in the living room and were quiet, Jane on one side and mother and daughter on the other.

David came by shortly, and said he had worked on tentative funeral arrangements.

"Gwen," he said. "Would you be able to tackle this tomorrow? I can be here first thing in the morning."

Laura answered for her. "Yes, we will."

Gwen didn't say anything but nodded. Laura and Jane were so glad to see that.

The next morning, David came and spoke to Gwen first.

"The funeral home in town will meet with us if you're up to going," he said.

Gwen didn't say anything for a few seconds. "I want to go," she said. She got up, grabbed her robe, and headed for the bathroom.

Jane let out a big sigh. "I think we're finally getting better," she said.

The local funeral director met with the group, and they planned the entire funeral. Kelly's body would be there Friday morning. The visitation would be at the funeral home on Friday night, and the service would be at the church on Saturday.

The navy would provide a full color guard and a gun salute. The Kansas Patriot Guard would escort and protect the route from protestors with their motorcycle group. Kelly's VFW would provide volunteers to help with traffic coordination.

Some admiral wanted to come and present a medal. David and Gwen really didn't know what that was for. But he was flying into McConnell Air Force Base near Wichita, and would drive to the funeral at the church.

Kelly's entire family, including his ex-wife, would be driving down on Friday. Gwen made plans for them to stay at the same bed-and-breakfast their families had stayed at for her and Kelly's wedding.

The visitation that Friday was packed. The funeral home wasn't large enough for a turnout this big. People formed a line that ran out of the funeral home and along the sidewalk in front of the building.

The receiving line included Gwen, her kids John, Laura & fiancé Ben. Kelly's first wife, Pat and their kids Jeanne, Josh & very pregnant fiancé Jen. Jane & David and their kids also stood with the large group.

After an hour, Gwen finally had to sit down. She was physically and mentally exhausted, and Jane knew it.

"I want to drive you home," said Jane. "There is plenty of family to man the receiving line."

Gwen didn't argue. She didn't have any more tears to cry.

Jane made sure Gwen was in bed before dark. The funeral would be even more arduous. It would start at ten in the morning.

At nine o'clock on Saturday morning, the funeral home limousine pulled into the driveway. Laura and Jane helped Gwen to the car. There was so much family around that the drive *to* the church looked like a funeral procession.

Kansas Patriot Guard motorcycles were at every intersection already. Local VFW members with brown jackets and brown caps coordinated traffic as the limousine and family member vehicles passed.

The small white steeple glistened brightly in the sunlight of the cold early February morning. People were already standing outside. Cars and pickups lined the gravel streets on all sides. The church lot where Kelly's fence stood was filling up with vehicles as fast as they could find a place to park. People who hadn't been back to the church since the extra parking lot and decorative fence had been redone, were amazed at how good it looked.

"There is no way we can seat everyone," said Gwen.

"We know that," said Jane. "David, church volunteers, and I set up chairs in the front area and in the fellowship room."

People were already sitting inside when the funeral party entered the building. The podium had been moved back almost to the wall. Family seating was set up sideways to the pews on the left side of the stage. The piano had been moved closer to the right side in the corner. The hallway to the Sunday school room was open for overflow mourners to stand.

Kelly's closed casket was on the right side of the platform, near where the piano usually stood. A picture of him in his dress blues stood in front of the piano on an easel. A small table was set up in front of the picture. There sat an empty flag case with all of Kelly's medals, angled for people to see. Josh had the case done by a Fort

Leavenworth military store, as a condolence request especially for the service.

At 10:05 a.m., David began the funeral. He told the attendees that people would be coming in and out several times during the service. He opened with prayer.

"Father in heaven, we are gathered here today to lay to rest our church member and friend Kelly Allen Raines." David went on with a very eloquent, proper prayer and message.

The funeral director had coordinated for two songs: "The Old Rugged Cross" and "Amazing Grace." There were no professional soloists, just attendees singing from the hymnals.

The admiral's group had insisted on standing outside on the porch. They had arrived at nine thirty, but all the seats were gone. People had offered their seats to him, but he refused politely, saying, "I will come in at the proper time to speak."

Following the music, David motioned for him to come forward. The dark blue uniform with its bright gold bars glistened as he walked to the front.

Josh was used to seeing his dad in uniform. Growing up, their family had gone to the reserve center many times. But he couldn't remember ever seeing an officer dressed this well.

"I am honored to be allowed to speak to you regarding this fine sailor, Mass Communications Specialist First Class Kelly Raines," said Rear Admiral John Derrick. "I have a letter from President George W. Bush to read to you."

Gwen opened her bloodshot eyes wide when she heard the president's name. As bad as she felt, pride rushed through her to have someone so important honor her husband.

"Dear Mrs. Raines and family: It was with the deepest sorrow that I learned of the passing of Kelly. May I extend my sincerest sympathy to you and all of your extended family. Kelly was the finest example of our nation's troops, and his sacrifice is respected and honored."

The admiral went on to read the rest of the president's letter. He also read portions of letters from the secretary of the navy, the chief of naval operations, and the governor of Kansas.

"Lastly, I want to finish with something that was well underway prior to Petty Officer Raines's death. On November tenth, MC1 Raines was involved in an IED explosion and terrorist attack."

Admiral Derrick read a description of the IED attack and battle.

"At great risk to his own life, and ignoring military protocol, Mass Communications Specialist First Class Kelly Raines ran from the safety of his vehicle and toward a downed Humvee. As he approached the disabled vehicle, five insurgents appeared from a cross street. Petty Officer Raines surprised them and opened fire, killing four terrorists and severely wounding a fifth. After taking wounds in his leg and abdomen, and as the vehicle flames and heat became worse, MC1 picked up and carried one surviving occupant back to his Humvee. He returned and carried a second survivor to a nearby Humvee, all the time receiving rounds to his protective vest and off his helmet. Both the victims he rescued and many other service members survived. They would not have done so without him.

"It is my greatest privilege to award Mass Communications Specialist First Class Kelly Raines, with the Navy Cross."

With that, the admiral walked by the casket to the small table set up in front of the picture and placed the bright medal on it. He backed up one step, put on his brilliant gold-and-white cap, and saluted.

The sight of the uniformed officer saluting, welded into everyone's memories. Tears ran down the face of almost everyone at the service. It was a moment that everyone in attendance, especially Josh, would forever remember.

My dad earned the Navy Cross, Josh thought. *I want to tell this story to my son someday.*

The service concluded, and the family group was immediately ushered out to the back Sunday school room. Funeral guests were allowed to pass by the casket and gaze at the picture and medal.

The pallbearers brought the casket out to the waiting hearse. Gwen had asked for Kelly's son, Laura's fiancé, Kelly's two brothers, and two of her brothers-in-law to be the pallbearers.

It was a short drive to the cemetery, just two miles north of Kelly and Gwen's farmhouse. The procession took some time to get underway. The traffic coordination by the Kansas Patriot Guard and the VFW veterans helped immensely.

At the cemetery, the hearse pulled alongside the large green tent. The pallbearers lifted the dark black casket and placed it over the bright aluminum rollers on top of the open grave. The family walked to the seating area, and the navy color guard and riflemen began their coordinated display. Wearing dress blues with brilliant white caps and gloves, the well-practiced team performed its part of the ceremony.

Next, an actual bugler played taps, followed by a seven-gun salute.

A navy flag team lifted the red, white, and blue flag and began the folding. An immaculately uniformed navy chief in his dress blue uniform with gold buttons and stripes handed the flag to Gwen.

"On behalf of a grateful nation, the president of the United States presents you with this flag in appreciation for your husband's sacrifice for his country."

Gwen accepted the flag with tears running down both cheeks. She didn't sob or have to be comforted. She bravely and respectfully resigned to the fact that she was a war widow.

She would never be the same. But the service had helped bring closure to this part of her life. Or so she thought.

CHAPTER 14

After Leigh accepted that she wasn't going to Kelly's funeral, she was finally able to come back to work. The days and weeks went by quickly as she tried to fit back into her old routine. But it wasn't the same. Kelly's death had ruined her deployment and military experience.

Before, she couldn't wait to get up and start her day, to tackle the latest story or get a good set of pictures and videos. Now she didn't want to get out of bed at all. This was a big change, for a girl who had always lit up the room for everyone.

Kelly had been her very best friend. They hadn't planned to become close or to have the affair. But it had happened just the same.

She couldn't help but notice that there was more going on with her health than depression.

Leigh looked at the calendar in her room. *I've missed a period!* she exclaimed to herself.

She went to bed that night feeling just as alone as if she weren't even married. *Bill would help me through this*, she thought.

Suddenly thoughts of her affair came flooding back, along with thoughts of Kelly's death. She had never felt so depressed in her life. *There is a reason war is so bad*, she thought. *There is nothing glamorous, heroic, or valiant about what I have been forced to endure.*

As the weeks passed, Leigh watched her calendar more closely when her second period should have started.

I think I might be pregnant, Leigh thought. *But that can't be*! She hadn't used any protection for years now. Surely if she were going to get pregnant, she would have before now.

Leigh decided she was going to have to see what was wrong. Besides the periods, her weight loss was obvious. Her clothes noticeably hung on her.

What is going on? she wondered. *Pregnant women gain weight.*

She felt as sad as she looked as she walked into the base medical office. Being pregnant, if she actually was, wasn't what she wanted, and she needed to find out for sure. She tore a number from the tab machine and sat down in the brown padded chairs.

How could a base this big not have home pregnancy test kits? she thought angrily. *I have to come here to do this.*

The doctor examination room was cold as Leigh sat on the bed, waiting for the results of her urine test. Her queasy stomach might just have been from lack of sleep and weight loss, she told herself. Morning sickness would be accompanied by throwing up, and she hadn't done that. So maybe she wasn't pregnant after all. And why would she be pregnant anyway? She had tried to get pregnant for years. How could it even be possible from an affair as brief as two days?

"Severe depression can bring on a loss of your menstrual cycle," the nurse had said.

She dreaded the repercussions if she was pregnant. She thought of telling Bill and what it would do to Gwen and all of Kelly's family. There was one thing she did know: abortion was out of the question.

If I am, then I'm keeping it, thought Leigh. *I don't know how I will deal with all the drama that would bring, but it will just have to be.* She and Bill had wanted a baby for far too long. And she still didn't think she could even possibly be pregnant.

She heard the nurse's voice in the hallway and then the doctor's steps heading toward her exam room. He knocked first and then came in. The accompanying nurse wasn't with him, so he left the door open.

"Well, you're pregnant," said the navy commander. "Now I need to see how much. We need to figure out your conception and delivery dates."

Leigh just sat there for a few seconds. Her severe depression coupled with the shock and emotional impact of being pregnant with another man's child hit her like a freight train. First her eyes widened. Then her heart pounded and she lost all ability to get ahold of herself. She turned away from the doctor and stared blankly at the wall.

The unit lead nurse came in and immediately recognized what had happened.

"All right. You, out," said the experienced army nurse.

The navy commander quickly left the exam room without speaking again.

"Let's just take a minute," said Burbanek, talking to Leigh. "I'll stay with you until you're ready to move on with the rest of what you will have to do. One step at a time."

They stayed that way for about a minute. Leigh was so depressed already. But if there was anything good about all of the prior tragedy, it did dull down some of the emotional shock. It was almost like God had said, let's take into account Kelly's death and let up some on this one.

Leigh finally shut her eyes and squeezed them tightly. First the tears came, running down both cheeks. Burbanek put her hand on Leigh's shoulder. Then Leigh began to shake her head, emotionally trying to get rid of the impact of all that was happening, all that had already happened.

Come on, girl, thought the lieutenant colonel. *Turn and look at me.* Without waiting for Leigh to look up, the army nurse reached around the ensign and hugged her hard.

That was it. Two and a half months of horrible depression and the news of today all came to the surface. Leigh sobbed slowly for a few seconds and then let it all out.

As her crying began to die down, the nurse tried to get to the bottom of why this pregnancy was so hard.

"What else happened here?" asked Burbanek. "Something besides this has you very upset."

"He died," sobbed Leigh. "He's gone." She immediately went back to hysterical screaming sobs.

"Who died?" asked Burbanek. "The father?"

Leigh nodded. The nurse looked at the ensign's wedding ring as she asked the next obvious question: "Are you married to someone else?"

"We both are," said Leigh, forgetting about past and present tenses.

"Was the father killed in action?" asked the nurse.

"Yes," said Leigh. "He died in an IED explosion."

"Ensign, I need to tell the doctor what I'm doing. Will you be all right for just a minute? I won't be gone long."

Leigh nodded as the nurse stepped out and closed the door. She was back in less than a minute.

Leigh was an emotional wreck. Her light coat of makeup was streaming down her face. Her eyes were red and swollen. She had no color in her face at all.

"Are you ready to proceed with the delivery date determination?" asked Burbanek. "We need to get that over with first."

Leigh nodded.

"When was your last period?" said Burbanek.

Leigh paused for a second, making a "wait a second" gesture with her hand. "Lieutenant colonel, I know exactly when I made love. It was a Friday and Saturday, and Kelly died that following Monday morning on January twentieth."

Leigh paused for a minute, but she didn't go back into hysterics. She took a deep breath, though, and proceeded to talk. "I haven't made love to anyone else here, prior to that or since. So whichever of those two days you want to pick, one of them would be accurate."

"That's close enough," said the nurse, "and *shh* on the father's name. You don't have to tell anyone, no matter what some officer may tell you. Sometimes these things can involve fraternization issues, and like I said, you don't have to tell a soul."

Well, we're past the hard part, for today anyway, thought Burbanek. The nurse got some more papers from her clipboard.

"You're going on three months along, so we're way behind on our prenatal work. The due date will be October 19. You can stay here in theater through the end of the week. Then you have to go back stateside. You're a reserve, is that right?"

"Yes," said Leigh.

"Then you will go through demobilization and return to your reserve center."

"Why can't I stay here longer than that?" asked Leigh. "I've been doing my job."

"It's a war theater," said the lieutenant colonel. "We have to send all the pregnant women back stateside. The active side can continue to work a shore station. But since you're a reservist, you don't have a shore billet to go back to. Policy says we have to demob you."

Leigh was a dedicated sailor and very accomplished in her job. The thought of being demobilized was professionally embarrassing, socially even more so.

"I'm going to send you to the obstetrics department," said Burbanek. "They will make an appointment for you to catch up on the prenatal work. It doesn't amount to a whole lot, so I advise you to get to a civilian OBGYN back home. They will do a much better job," she said.

"Also, I want you to come back here tomorrow, just to talk," said Burbanek. "We have an opening at"—she looked at her schedule—"1400. Here is my number at the hospital. If you ever need someone to confide in, I have a lot of experience with this." The lieutenant colonel wrote her contact number on a note and handed it to Leigh.

"Thank you," said Leigh. As she got up, she reached out to hug the head nurse.

Leigh picked up the hall telephone and called her PAO command to send the duty driver to pick her up. When she walked into the office, Senior Chief Wilson was watching for her to come in. She took one look at Leigh's pale face and immediately walked up to her.

"Ensign, you don't have to work the rest of the day. Go back to your can and come in tomorrow."

Leigh didn't argue and turned to see if she could still catch the duty driver. He was still waiting in front of the building, watching the front door. When she came outside and opened the passenger door, the driver said, "Take you back to the cans?"

Leigh nodded and sat down. *We certainly have no secrets here*, she thought to herself. The driver never asked or tried to pry information out of her in any way. He politely drove her right to her door.

Leigh couldn't eat any supper. She was pregnant, and the father wasn't her husband. There had been no R&R for her to even see Bill, let alone make love to him. No way could she even think about pulling that old trick.

She decided to call him. It would probably make things worse for her, but waiting to give news like this wasn't accomplishing anything.

Bill would be getting ready for work. Her stomach was in knots, but she could take charge when something needed to be done.

The phone rang twice before he picked up.

"Bill—" That was all Leigh could get out.

"What's the matter, honey?" he asked.

Leigh still couldn't talk.

"Leigh, if you need to take some time and call me back, that's fine," he said.

"No," said Leigh. "I—" She paused again, trying to get ahold of herself. "Bill, I'm pregnant!"

Bill paused at hearing that.

"I've had an affair, and now I'm pregnant," said Leigh.

This time Bill couldn't speak for a minute, but he finally did. "Leigh—" And that was all he could get out.

Her quiet sobs began to get to him, and he started to cry. They just stayed on the phone that way for another minute, both of them crying together.

"Who's the guy?" Bill was finally able to ask.

"It's Kelly," said Leigh, "but I'm just as responsible as he is."

Bill didn't say anything for a few seconds. Leigh immediately had the deep want that every cheating spouse encounters.

"Bill, I want to stay married to you, if you will let me."

Again Bill didn't say a word.

"I want to say something else too. Bill, I am having and keeping this baby. I want you to be the father, if you will."

This time Bill started to cry. They paused again for a minute. Then Bill hung up. There was no slamming down of the receiver, just the click of the connection.

Leigh sat on the other end of the line, listening to the awful sound she hadn't heard since a caller into her TV station had hung up on her before she left for her deployment.

Leigh cried for a while in the phone booth. Then she wiped her tears away, got up, and walked outside. *I know Bill is walking*, she thought.

She knew she shouldn't be surprised by his reaction. But it hurt just the same.

Leigh tossed and turned all night, but surprisingly she got some sleep. At the office the next day, she went to see Senior Chief Wilson shortly after arriving.

"Senior, I need to go back to the hospital again this afternoon."

"That's fine," said Wilson. "You just go when you need to. All we really have going is the editing of the stories due out by the end of the week. If you can make some headway on those, well, there will be less to do tomorrow."

"Be glad to, Senior."

Wilson looked at her for a second. "Leigh, if you need to talk, about anything, I'm here."

Leigh knew the senior chief had figured out everything, again. She was a very good friend and shipmate.

"Thank you, Senior. I think probably later this afternoon."

Wilson knew exactly what she meant. "Sounds good, Ensign."

Leigh had the duty driver drop her off for her appointment.

"Do you know what time you will need to be picked up?" asked the driver.

"I don't know how long I'll be," said Leigh. "But I'll call if I need a ride. Thank you, John," Leigh said as she touched his arm. *My shipmates have been so good to me*, she thought.

She walked up to the front desk. The head nurse was there, talking to her coworkers. Lieutenant Colonel Burbanek took her to a vacant exam room and began to talk.

"How we doing this afternoon?" she asked.

"I finally did go to sleep," said Leigh.

"All you have to deal with can overwhelm you," said Burbanek. "But only if you let it. The best thing is to take one step at a time. And when life begins to become too much, just slow down and go right back to that one step at a time approach."

Leigh nodded.

"Well first, what are you going to do with the baby?"

"I am having and keeping this baby!" declared Leigh.

"That's what I want to hear," said Burbanek. "The health and love for it are number one. When are you going to tell your husband?"

"I called him last night," said Leigh.

"How did it go?" asked the nurse. "Is he still there?"

"He took it pretty bad," said Leigh. "He finally hung up on me."

"Well, you were honest and sincere," said Burbanek. "That's the most important thing." She didn't say that infidelity almost always breaks up military marriages. "There will be many more hard spots to come," the nurse added. "But if both people want to make the marriage survive the affair, you have a chance."

"I want to stay," said Leigh. "Bill is the one I'm worried about."

"He's the one you *should* be worried about," said Burbanek. "If there is anything good about the father being passed away, it's that you don't have to deal with him. But you may have to deal with his family when they find out. Were you close to them?"

"Not real close, but we knew each other. I talked to his wife on the phone. We met once."

Leigh changed the subject. She wanted to ask some questions. "Colonel, I don't understand how I could have gotten pregnant, how any man could have gotten me pregnant."

"Were you using birth control before with your husband?" asked the nurse.

"No, we never did. I had endometriosis, and my OBGYN said that was probably the reason I couldn't conceive."

"Well, what about the husband?" Burbanek said. "He needed to be tested too."

"He went at first," Leigh said. "But Bill didn't want to provide the samples."

The accomplished army nurse thought for a bit. "I'm just speculating," she said. "But I'm guessing that the baby's father was a healthy man, capable of impregnating any woman?"

Leigh's mind immediately flashed back to her and Kelly's lovemaking session against the storeroom wall. Her eyes opened wide as she remembered Kelly's bulging muscles, as he held her against the bulkhead.

The nurse went on to say that low sperm counts were much more common than people realized. "Your husband could still be tested," Burbanek said, "if you still want to know."

Leigh didn't even want to bring that up with Bill.

"What have you told your command?"

"I haven't," said Leigh. "But they've probably figured it out. I've been here twice now."

"Well, if you don't tell them, I have too. Can you do that? Are you dealing with all of this well enough to take that step in the next day or two?"

"Let me walk back and get it all ready to say," said Leigh. "I might even be able to tell them today."

Leigh headed out of the hospital and began a slow walk back to her PAO office. The spring temperatures were starting to warm up. The wind blew her hair as she put on her cover.

She thought of Kelly's wife, Gwen, and their combined four kids that he was so proud of. She thought of Bill, their folks, and all of the people this was going to affect.

Leigh thought of her childhood and how she had grown up always wanting to know her father and to be around his other family.

It was cruel that Leigh's grandmother had refused to let her see her dad. Even her mother had completely shunned her father when the teen pregnancy had come to light. Leigh's grandmother had never spoken to her father again.

The man had married and had other children, ones with whom she was never allowed to play. Leigh couldn't grow up with them or have the sibling relationships other families had, especially with the stepsister who looked and was so much like her.

I don't want this baby to be raised like that, thought Leigh. *There has to be a way.*

Leigh, her dad, and her stepsister had a very close relationship now, one Leigh was determined she would provide for her baby. But she didn't quite know what to do about Kelly's family learning of the pregnancy and eventual delivery.

They will eventually find out, Leigh thought. "*It will be just like Army Nurse Burbanek told me.*

Her baby would have nieces and nephews that could and should be playmates too. There would be a full realm of family, directly related. She would just have to figure that problem out.

Leigh worried that the baby wouldn't even know a father at all, if Bill didn't want to stay.

As Leigh neared her office, she was surprised that she hadn't thought at all about what was going to happen to her in Iraq. At the front door, her feet somehow steered their way toward the skipper's office.

"Hi, Debbie," said Leigh to Captain Benton's aide. Debbie was an E-3 and was striking for the MC rate.

"Hey, Leigh," said Debbie as she looked up with genuine care and concern.

"Does the skipper have a minute?" Leigh asked.

"I'll ask," said Debbie. "I think he will."

The captain's aide walked into his open office and pulled the door almost shut. She went straight up to his desk without stopping.

"Skipper," said Debbie. "It's the ensign."

"Send her right in," said Benton as he picked up his paperwork and set it to the side.

Debbie came back to the door. "He can see you right now," she said, holding it open.

Leigh could see tears starting down Debbie's cheeks as she walked past. Captain Benton didn't even get to say, "How are you doing?" Debbie's tears had started Leigh's flowing, and when Leigh looked up at the skipper, she lost it.

He had already asked the senior chief to come in if the ensign asked to see him. Wilson had seen Leigh come in. The senior chief had started making her way across the quarterdeck, as soon as Debbie stepped back into the doorway.

Without saying a word to Debbie or the captain, the senior chief walked right into the office and put her arms around Leigh. Debbie pulled the door shut.

For several seconds the two women just stood like they were. The captain just sat behind his desk, waiting for the right time to speak. This time the women didn't go into loud sobbing at all. They just cried quietly. After a long minute, they sat down in two chairs already set up in front of the skipper's desk.

Leigh was the first to speak. "I'm pregnant," she said, teary eyed and struggling to deal with her now public humiliation. "I have to demob by the end of the week."

Captain Benton stepped up with his very best professional leadership. "What can I do to make this as easy on you as possible?" he asked.

"Well, there's nothing wrong with me," said Leigh. "I can certainly work through the next few days."

"That's fine with me," said Benton.

"She can work, but it has to be here," said Wilson. "She's not going out on any convoys."

"Ordered and done," stated Benton sternly.

They went on to complete the demobilization. Debbie came back in and helped with the flight arrangements and coordinated Leigh's trunk shipping through the post office. She would fly out of the AACG-DACG at 0200 hours on Thursday.

Leigh didn't have a lot of stuff in her can. She had bought very little at the exchange. She did have a refrigerator and coffeemaker. Leigh made up a For Sale sign, and put it up on the PAO bulletin board. Both items were spoken for within two hours.

Later that day she went back to her can to pack. She paused to look at the walls for a bit. These cans had been home for six months. She had pictures of Bill, the cats, and her niece. A few of her published stories were on the desk.

Leigh brought out her gorilla box trunks and began to load them. Next, she brought out her sea and flight bags and packed them with what she wouldn't need for the rest of the week.

Debbie had arranged for the duty driver to pick up her mail home trunks and boxes on Wednesday. Leigh rode with him to the post office and mailed them to Ohio.

By late afternoon on Wednesday, she had everything stowed away. Her uniform for the next day was laid out. She headed to the galley to eat her last meal. If she slept until midnight, she would have enough time to dress and meet the duty driver from the watch.

At 0030 hours, she began to drag all of her bags to the pickup point. Senior Chief Wilson's light was on, and she came out to help Leigh with her bags.

"I thought you would be headed out about now," said Wilson. She reached out and picked up Leigh's CBR pack. They walked together to the pickup point.

"It was nice that the armory let me check in my M16 and pistol," said Leigh. "I hope I never have to lug a big gun around again."

Then, without even thinking, she began to cry again. Wilson cried with her as the two women stood waiting for the truck. Soon the headlights of an oncoming vehicle turned the corner and stopped beside them.

"You have my numbers," said Wilson as she hoisted Leigh's stuff into the back of the bed.

"I'll call," said Leigh.

The two women hugged one last time, and Leigh got in the passenger side of the small pickup.

CHAPTER 15

The flight from Al-Asad to Kuwait was on a small air force cargo and troop carrier plane. When they landed in Kuwait, Leigh carried her bags into the holding area. She was demobilizing with several Seabee women and would stay in their quarters.

Leigh loaded her stuff onto a bus and rode to Seabee Camp Moreell. There, she was assigned to a barracks with the other women. They would check in the SAPI plates from their MTV vests. Leigh would fly out in two days.

She spent what was left of the night in a sixteen-bed bunkhouse. Only four other women were there. She knew the morning would be a good time to call Bill and tried to think about what she was going to say to him this time. She lay awake, dreading the call. She hadn't talked to him since Monday. Even though she had never called more than once a week before, their relationship was all different now.

At 0500, she got up, showered, and headed for the MWR phone bank. There was only one other sailor there. She dialed the numbers and punched in her phone card pin. Soon the phone was ringing. It was 9 p.m. at night in Ohio.

"Hello," said Bill as he answered the phone on the first ring.

"Hi, Bill," said Leigh. "I'm in Kuwait. We came in last night."

"I don't want to talk to you," he said.

Leigh paused and started to cry. No one said anything for almost a minute.

"Bill," Leigh asked, "would you try?"

Then Bill finally spoke. He had been thinking over everything and thought it was time for his wife to hear what he wanted to say.

"No," he said. "I won't. Leigh, I've found another place to stay. I'm moving out this week."

Leigh was devastated at hearing that news. But she was a strong girl and wasn't afraid to fight for something if she wanted it.

"I'm not going to accept that," Leigh said sternly. "I won't, Bill."

"Well, you're going to have to," he answered.

"Where are you going?" she asked. "Who in your family can stand to live with you?"

"I'm not moving in with anybody!" he said.

"Are you getting an apartment in that rundown complex by your work?" Leigh asked.

"Let me worry about that," Bill answered.

"Bill, you don't make enough money to stay there," Leigh said. "You would have to eat on a bare bones grocery budget. If your car breaks down, what would you do then?"

"Leigh," said Bill, "I'm leavin'. I've told you twice now. I'm going to say good-bye." Bill cried hard when he said it, but he got the word *good-bye* out.

As much as it hurt, Leigh knew her husband. She heard the phone hang up, and she took her turn on the crying towel.

On the second day, she packed her things to fly out. A large bus would take them to Kuwait City Airport to fly back to the states. Leigh carried her bags to the pickup point. Several Seabees who were also leaving, loaded her bags into the luggage compartment under the bus.

The ride to Kuwait City Airport took just over an hour. The Seabees immediately unloaded the bags, and the group headed into the military terminal.

The small group waited for most of the day for the commercial flight that would take them back to the states. Late in the afternoon, they loaded their stuff onto the baggage truck. The civilian KBR workers took the checked luggage to the plane. Then the group got onto another bus and headed toward the waiting plane.

Leigh shouldered her carry-on bags and walked up the ramp and onto the big white World Airlines jet. It had been a while since she had seen American flight stewards. Military from all branches of the service filed onto the plane. Civilian workers flew out as well.

She sat in a window seat for the long flight. They would have a stopover again in Germany and then head on to Norfolk. She closed her eyes to try to sleep for a while.

The stopover in Germany was short. She didn't buy anything at the duty free shops.

The flight to Norfolk didn't seem that long, even though it was ten additional hours.

It was early evening eastern standard time as the plane set down on the Naval Station Oceana runway.

Leigh grabbed her carry-on bags and waited outside the plane for her checked luggage to be distributed. Then she boarded the waiting bus and rode to the main naval base in Norfolk.

It was close to eight when Leigh carried all of her luggage into her room. She decided not to call Bill, but she did activate her cell phone.

Leigh went through all of the demobilization procedures. They usually took about four days. Because of her pregnancy, she spent quite a bit of time at medical. The demobilization team she was assigned to kept track of her at all times. On the morning of the fourth day, the staff yeoman booked her flight back to Ohio.

She called a cab and rode to the civilian airport in Norfolk. The flight home included a plane change in Washington, DC. As she got on the connecting flight, she realized she was going to her home airport and no one would be there to meet her.

During the entire flight, she dreaded the hurt she had caused Bill. She also had to deal with her television career. *I don't know how I can live down an affair pregnancy on public TV*, she thought. *I may not keep my morning show job.* But she was determined to live through the humiliation and to push through all of the problems to come.

Her plane touched down. She forced herself out of her seat. *Here we go*, she said to herself. As she walked out of the gate and toward the baggage claim, she instinctively looked for Bill. A hollow hurt came through her even though she had known he wouldn't be there. Tears rolled down her face, but not for long. Leigh swallowed hard and went to the luggage carousel to wait for her checked bags.

She called a cab to take her to their house. She did have her house and office keys in her purse, which she had taken out of her gorilla box in Virginia. The driver let her out at home and helped her carry her bags to the door. He wouldn't let her give him a tip when he turned to walk back to the cab, and he waited to make sure she got in her door.

An eerie quiet hung in the air as she opened the front door. She brought her bags in and looked around the living room. Everything was just as she had left it.

What did he take with him? she wondered. Leigh walked into the kitchen and then the bedroom. The kitchen table, dishes, pots and pans, and everything in the bedroom were still there. She opened the closet. Most of his clothes were gone.

I wonder if he took the guest bed. Leigh opened the door to the second bedroom, and it was exactly like she had left it too. "What is he sleeping on?" Leigh exclaimed.

She knew he wouldn't take the washer and dryer, but she still looked in the laundry room. It was all was there. *I guess I could see if I have a car*, she thought. Leigh opened the side door to the garage, and there was her SUV. Bill had left her everything. And his car wasn't much.

A little before six in the evening, Leigh got her phone out of her purse and called her husband. "What are you sleeping on?" she asked as Bill said hello. "Do you have any furniture?"

Bill had been going without sleep, was barely eating, and had basically been miserable since he found out about Leigh's affair and pregnancy. He hadn't been doing all that well with her deployment in general, even before all this happened.

He started crying and couldn't talk for a bit. Leigh was quick to pick up on that.

"Bill, are you all right?" she asked.

Bill got ahold of himself enough to answer. "I'm fine," he finally got out.

"Bill," Leigh said, "I'm bringing you the guest bed. I don't know what you're sleeping on, but it can't be good. And I'm bringing you some furniture and kitchen items."

Bill didn't pause long before answering. "Leigh, I don't want to see you. I can get my own stuff."

Leigh knew that meant he didn't have anything, probably just some cot and an electric skillet.

"What apartment are you in?" she asked.

Bill didn't answer.

"Bill, I need to know your address sometime. I will have to forward your mail."

Bill hadn't thought about that. "I'm in apartment 204 in the Westside Villa," he said. "But I don't want you to bring anything, just forward the mail."

"Okay," Leigh answered. She said good-bye and hung up. *I am taking him a load of stuff tomorrow*, she determined, *if I can get him to accept it.*

Leigh unpacked the rest of her clothes. She tried to eat some canned food she opened up, but she wasn't very hungry. She ate enough to be able to sleep, alone, without her man.

The next day, Leigh called their pastor and asked to see him. The minister said that Bill had talked to him and told him everything.

Her car keys were on the hook in the kitchen. She drove for the first time in almost nine months. The minister was waiting for her when she knocked on the parsonage door.

"Hello there, Miss Leigh," he said as he opened the door. She immediately gave him a big hug. "Have a seat and tell me how all is going," he said.

"It's not," she answered. "Bill left me, or is trying too anyway."

"He told me he had decided to leave," Evans said. "How hard was that for you?"

Leigh broke down and, for the second time, went all to pieces.

She wasn't the only spouse the minister had counseled, although it was unusual for the blamed spouse to be a woman. He waited patiently for her to calm down.

"You're not over the hard part yet," he said. "Almost all of the spouses leave, or eventually do."

"He isn't going to make it financially," said Leigh. "He left everything with me, his apartment has nothing, and he is driving a barely reliable car," she said.

"I suspected that," Evans said. "But let's worry about you and the baby for now. How about prenatal care?"

"I will make an appointment with an OBGYN today," she said.

"Leigh," the minister said, "forgive me, but you look terrible. Your health isn't good. This much weight loss is a danger to the baby, not to mention you."

Leigh looked her pastor right in the eye as he said that. The words scared her to death.

"Would you do something for me?" he asked. "I want you to go to lunch with me. I'm famished, and there is a good buffet on James Street."

Leigh wasn't a bit hungry, but she agreed to go. The minister thought if he could get some food down her, at least that would help avoid the miscarriage he feared could come.

They got to the local Golden Corral just before eleven in the morning. At the pastor's insistence, Leigh did eat a decent meal. She even went back to get dessert. They continued to talk over what Leigh could do, and she filled the minister in on all that had happened in Iraq.

As she prepared to go, she told her minister about her job fears. "I don't think the station will keep me," she said. "I will be the talk all over Columbus."

The pastor thought for a bit and replied. "You don't know that," he said. "Celebrities do worse things than this all the time."

She promised to call an OBGYN as she left the restaurant, and already she felt much better. Back at the house, she looked up several doctors, and the first one she called agreed to see her at the end of the week. Next Leigh looked at the kitchen, thought about the spare bed, and decided she was going to do what her pastor would certainly prefer her not to.

I am taking a load to Bill, she thought. *including the guest bed.*

Leigh borrowed their neighbor's lawn mower trailer, found the trailer hitch she had never used, put it into her bumper receiver, and hooked the trailer onto it. She backed it up to her garage, and the first thing she loaded was the bed. Leigh put in the frame first and then the box springs and mattress. Then she grabbed two empty totes and filled them with pots, pans, and a china set. Leigh finished by filling another tote with cupboard staples and then closed the trailer tailgate.

She drove straight to Bill's so-called apartment. The apartment manager was outside the office when Leigh pulled through two parking spaces to talk to him.

"Are you the girl that used to be on the Channel 2 morning show?" asked the surprised manager.

"Yes," Leigh said. "I've been deployed with the navy overseas for a while."

"Are you moving in?" he asked.

"Nope," she said. "Just trying to bring some furniture and items to my husband. We separated."

The apartment manager wasn't surprised at all. He had many tenants going through marital changes like this. "Since he isn't here," he said, "would I be right if I guessed he didn't know you were comin'?"

"Yep," Leigh said. "Is there any chance I could get you to let me put the items inside for him?"

The manager looked at her for a second. "What's going to happen if I let you do that?" he asked. "How good is your man to get along with?"

"He's probably sleeping on some camper cot," she said. "He wouldn't be someone to raise hell with you. He won't even do that with me." Leigh paused for a second. "He will finally go ahead and use the stuff," she said. "If you're worried about it ending up out in the parking lot, Bill wouldn't be like that."

At the mention of his name, the manager suspected who Bill probably was. "Is this Bill Andrews?" he asked.

"Yes," said Leigh.

"Well, he's in 204. Back your trailer in right there. You don't have much, so I'll help you carry it up the stairs."

Leigh was thankful for the help, and the two set the bed and totes inside the apartment living room. She had brought some of Bill's clothes in a suit bag. They left that inside too.

Leigh was careful not to set up the bed, but she did look around to see how Bill was living. *There's the cot*, she said to herself. *The kitchen looks like he is using the microwave to cook with.* Leigh had made sure there was a can opener with the table service she had brought. Now Bill had spatulas, a mixing whip, and a few other cooking utensils.

"Are you sure he's going to be good about this?" the manager asked again.

"He won't say a word to either you or me," Leigh said. "He might not set up the bed right away, but I'm hoping he will. Are you okay with me coming to see him soon?" Leigh asked.

"I have 'exes come here all the time," he said. "You and Bill look like you will be agreeable folks. I hope it stays that way, for both of you."

Leigh thanked the manager and headed home. *Bill will have his moment when he sees this*, she thought. *But he is living one step above homelessness!*

Bill got home from work at his usual time. He had stopped at the grocery store and picked up a meatloaf dinner to heat up. He opened the door and immediately saw all the things Leigh had brought him.

"God-damn-it," said Bill. "I don't want this stuff!"

He walked past everything. He knew Leigh had talked the motel manager into letting her in.

He opened his store-bought dinner, put it on the microwave plate, and set it for four minutes. He struggled to continue with his routine, but his thoughts were only of Leigh. He missed her terribly. He just didn't think he could accept that she had cheated on him. An even worse hurt was that he hadn't been able to get her pregnant, and Kelly could. He felt impotent, inadequate, and that his wife had traded up for someone better.

As he ate, he couldn't help but look at the totes and bed. *I guess I could set up the bed*, he thought. He washed his few dishes, took down his fold-up cot, and grabbed the bed frame. Soon, he had it set up. Bill looked to see if there were any sheets and blankets in the totes. He found several sets, including pillows and pillow cases.

Later that night, he grumbled as he struggled to go to sleep. *This sure feels better than the cot*, he thought. Soon Bill was sleeping soundly and got the best night's sleep he'd had since he moved out of their home.

CHAPTER 16

The next morning, Leigh called her station manager to say she was back. She asked to come see him. Phil Benson had been Leigh's boss for years, and he was surprised to hear her voice. She was supposed to be deployed for a year. He immediately knew something was wrong.

"Is everything all right?" he asked.

"No," replied Leigh. "I need to come in person. When is a good time?"

"We have advertising staff meetings already set for later this morning," Phil said. "Come by midafternoon, and I will move some things that can wait till tomorrow."

Leigh drove to the station and took a deep breath as she got out of the car. Her coworkers were surprised to see her.

Phil had worked for the station for going on twenty years. He had been there when Leigh was hired and very much enjoyed working with her. Unlike Leigh, Phil had never been in the military. While he didn't exercise with navy physical training programs like Leigh, he was still as slender as when he had been on camera every day. The man bicycled all the time, after work and on weekends.

Phil was a very good station manager. Since he had taken over, the station had stayed in the black financially almost every month. He had worked especially hard with the advertising department, and they now had an excellent sales record. Bringing Leigh to the morning show originally had been his idea, and he very much wanted her to come back to work after deployment.

Phil asked her to come into his office as soon as she arrived. He hugged his long-time coworker and waited for her to say what was going on.

"I'm pregnant," said Leigh. "I had an affair in Iraq, and I'm going on four months along."

Phil just sat in his chair. He was in shock. He watched her tear up and cry quietly.

"I'm not sure what the right thing is to say," Phil said. "I want to be supportive. What can I do?"

"Well, I want to keep my job," Leigh said. "Is there anything you can do about that?"

"I want you to keep your job too," Phil said. Leigh's boss sat quietly for a few seconds, obviously thinking what he wanted to do. "I will have to run this by the owners. But don't expect the worst. We've never handled anything quite like this."

Phil and Leigh had worked together for more than ten years. He had briefly shared the morning show with her, before promoting into the evening anchor and later the station manager position.

He and Leigh talked briefly about their experiences and her family. Then Leigh went home, knowing this was probably the end of her TV news career.

Leigh went home from her job visit determined that she was going to get two hard things over in the same day. She figured Bill would be home by six in the evening. She didn't think he would talk on the phone.

I am going to see him, she told herself.

Leigh knew Bill would be inside his apartment at exactly the same time every day. As she drove up to the parking lot, she saw his car, so she parked her SUV right beside it and walked up to the second deck door.

She tried to fight back the tears as she got close, but even strong willed as she was, Leigh was still an emotional human being like everyone else. She knocked on the door, but no sound came from the other side.

"Bill, let me in," she blubbered. "Bill, please!"

Leigh waited for a long minute, until Bill finally decided to open the door. The two just looked at each other, both crying, before Leigh finally spoke.

"Can we talk?" she asked. "I will leave whenever you want me to go."

Bill didn't say anything. His hand shook as he gripped the door. Finally, he moved aside and opened it. The kitchen chairs were close by, so she walked over to one and stood by it. Her totes were still there, although they had been opened and a few things had been taken out.

Bill sat down in a chair first, followed by Leigh. Leigh was trying to get Bill to talk first to see if she could get him to get it off his chest. At least she could make that much headway with her husband today.

Bill finally complied. "Leigh, how could you?" he said. Then all he could do was cry.

Leigh hadn't thought about it before, but Bill had self-esteem problems. He had all his life. He'd always been smaller than other men. He was balding and had learned the very hard way that he wasn't able to get Leigh pregnant. Leigh decided to take just one step at a time.

"Bill," she said, "blame me. I'm the one who gave in, who cheated on you."

"Well, how did you do it? I never thought something like this would ever happen, especially from you."

"We never planned it or flirted beforehand," Leigh said. "Kelly got shot up and then I just missed being blown up. Nothing makes it right, but it happened."

"How many times?" he asked.

"It was over two days. I came back from my near miss, and it was that night and the next day. I ended it then, and our command pitched holy hell over it."

"How did you get pregnant?" Bill asked.

"The army nurse and I think Kelly's sperm count was healthy and normal, and the affair happened to time my cycle right. We also think your sperm count is low. We would have found that out if you had been tested before by the doctor," Leigh said.

Bill shook his head.

"It doesn't make you less of a man, Bill," Leigh said. "You were and are the finest of husbands."

"What are you going to do now?" Bill interrupted.

"Bill, I am having and keeping this baby!"

Bill struggled to keep up with what was coming. He was a present person who generally just worried about today. He didn't spend a lot of time planning for the future, or for anything past tomorrow for that matter.

Leigh thought she should stop there. They had at least gotten this far. She changed the subject. "I'm sorry I went into your apartment without telling you," she said. "There are many more things at the house that you should have."

"This is plenty," Bill said.

When Leigh got up to go, they didn't touch or even say good-bye. After she stepped outside, she heard him shut the door behind her.

Leigh was home the next day when the station manager called her on her cell phone.

"Leigh, I want you to come into the station," he said. "I've met with the owners and I want to go over all of this with you."

"Phil," she said. "I'm a big girl. Tell me what they said. I can deal with it."

The station manager didn't want to do this over the phone and argued with Leigh for a bit, but he finally gave in.

"It's a no on going back on the air," he said, "at least for now. They—we don't know exactly what we want to do about everything. But we want you to come back to work."

"Doing what?" Leigh asked.

"Leigh, just listen for a minute. I want you to help me with station management, to share my duties, which have been way too many for a long time now. I know you well enough to insist that you seriously consider this."

Leigh appreciated his sincerity. And she knew she didn't deserve to have any type of job offer at all.

"I want to be a part of the station," she said, "and I don't deserve to go back on the air for what I've done. Will the other employees and owners accept me?"

"Yes, they will," he said. "Oh, you will probably get some stares, but I think you are tough enough to endure and move past that."

They went on to talk about her new duties and the maternity leave she would have to plan for. Leigh was just glad to have a job. The station didn't have to do this for her, and she was so thankful that they were.

The next day, Leigh went into the office to go over her new job.

"I want you to key on advertising coordination," Phil said. "I can't keep up with all of it."

He described he would handle all of the morning show and evening news spots but she would coordinate the day and weekend advertising.

"What about the content?" Leigh asked. Content was news or features the station would use during the airtime. Spots were sold advertising.

"I will have you help with that eventually," he said "Let's chase the money first."

Phones had rung throughout the station offices since Leigh had come inside.

"There are too many advertising calls to deal with them all promptly, he said. "I will ask you to follow my lead and let me transfer the ones I want to you. The bigger the ad, the sooner you and I will talk to them. In time, I want you to begin making decisions. You will know what to bring to me."

Phil got up and Leigh followed him down the hallway.

"Your office will be right here," Phil said as he showed her the empty room. "This isn't nice, but I think you can make it presentable."

Leigh looked around at the dull room. There was a dust-covered desk and several boxes of unwanted items other employees had stored there.

"There isn't any remodeling money," Phil said. "You'll have to do that on your own."

Leigh went to work on it. She found the custodian closet, brought up the broom, dust pan, and mop, and spent the rest of the morning and part of the afternoon locating furniture from the station basement. She soon had something decent to work in.

Leigh connected with the information technician for computer and telephone access. IT would have it all ready by the next day.

The following morning, she brought in desktop and office items from home. She bought her own stationary, mouse pad, and wall decorations. Now she could get started.

CHAPTER 17

Leigh waited two days before she called Bill again. She thought he would answer the phone, and he did.

"Bill," she said. "Would you meet with me again to talk?"

Bill was quiet. Leigh was certainly used to that from him.

"Come here tomorrow, to the house," Leigh said.

"What are we going to talk about?" he asked

"Well," Leigh replied, "I need to tell you about my job and the house, and grovel to try to get you to come back home." Leigh couldn't stop the tears this time, and she had to pause.

Bill was doing the same thing, though he tried to keep her from knowing it. He decided to speak. "I'll come," he said. "But just to talk. I don't want to come back home."

Leigh expected that and swallowed hard so she could speak.

"I will be at work for part of the day," she said. "Come after you get off work. I will have something for supper."

"All right," Bill answered.

Friday afternoon, Leigh cooked a simple dinner of soup, salad, and bread. She heard Bill's car pull into the driveway. He walked up and knocked on the door instead of coming in. Leigh walked over to let him in. She didn't try to hug or kiss him or push him along at all.

"Come in and sit down at the table," she said. "Everything is ready."

They ate quietly, and Leigh prepared to say what she felt was right. After supper, she got right to it.

"I lost my job on the morning show, but I'm still at the TV station," she said. "I have a station assistant manager job now."

"Did they decide to take you off the air for the pregnancy?" asked Bill.

"Yes, I think so. I took that risk anyway when I deployed, if you remember me talking about it. But I told them everything, and Phil asked me to stay on as his assistant. He implied that he and the owners had been considering me for this for some time."

Bill didn't say anything. He was obviously thinking. Leigh decided to ask the hard question now.

"Bill, what do you want to do, with us? Do you want to legally separate, begin divorce proceedings? What do you want to do about me?"

Bill didn't like what he was hearing. He really just wanted to get up and leave, to walk like he had done before when he'd had to face a hard thing in life. But he didn't do that this time.

"I don't know what I want to do," he replied. Tears began to fill his eyes.

Leigh's eyes filled up in return as she sat looking at her husband. She decided to bring up the pregnancy. "There is a baby coming. What do you want to do about that?"

"It's not mine!" he blurted out.

Leigh paused for a second. She knew Bill couldn't be pushed much more. "Bill, I want you to forgive me more than anything, to come back home and be here for me. But that will include fatherhood!"

Bill didn't say anything. He stopped crying. Then he got up and spoke. "Leigh, I want to go now."

Leigh knew this was the time to stop, and she did. She didn't say another word or even good-bye. She stood as Bill walked to the door, quietly opened it, and walked away.

Leigh could hear his old car starter, the transmission shifting gears, and then the faintness of the motor sound as it faded away.

Leigh went back to work the next morning, and settled into her new role at the television station. Word about the affair quietly made its way around the office, as well as through family and community social circles. Leigh even told a few coworkers the truth, that she had an affair and that the father was killed in the war.

She met with Phil several times, and he helped her get set and take on advertising and some programming content calls.

If you have to choose between content and advertising, he had said, *take the money calls every time.*

Most of the employees didn't stare or talk about her situation. She asked the people who did bring up the baby, to help her get through all that had happened, and told them she wanted to be a good mother to her firstborn. Her boss and coworkers supported her and offered to help in any way.

That evening, Leigh went home and thought of Bill. *I wish he would try,* she thought. *Maybe if something bad would happen, he would come to help me.* But nothing like that happened. Leigh was a healthy, strong girl. Her pregnancy was proceeding very well, better now that she was eating properly.

On Saturday, Leigh decided to get another hard part over while she had the time.

She drove to Bill's parents' home. As she walked to the front door, nervous anxiety overwhelmed her, but she made herself knock.

Bill's mom, Barbara, opened the door and didn't say a word. Leigh stood there crying and finally asked to come in. Barbara hugged Leigh briefly and called to her husband, Tom, to come into the living room. Tom walked over to hug Leigh as well.

Leigh told them the same thing she had told her boss and coworkers, that she'd had an affair, was pregnant, and—if Bill would have her—was going to have and raise the baby.

Tom was the first to speak. "Leigh, Bill may not be able to do this," he said. "I don't know that I could."

Leigh sat for a bit before she answered. "That may be," she said. "But I am going to try."

She didn't stay long.

I'm not here to get Bill's folks to talk him into coming back, Leigh said to herself.

She thanked them for seeing her, said good-bye, and drove back home.

Bill was just as miserable. He hated his apartment, his cooking, and living by himself. He missed his wife terribly. Bill wanted to forgive her and accept what had happened. But it was not an easy thing to do. He was very hurt by the affair, which was multiplied by the fact that another guy had been able to get her pregnant.

Bill had become used to being the smaller man in the room. But he was always very proud to walk into a public place with Leigh by his side. She turned heads, and she had been his, something Bill could show off. How would he ever do that again? *Everyone will know she had an affair and is now pregnant*, he thought.

Driving home from work, Bill looked at the street he was on. He had done it again. He had driven toward their house instead of his apartment. He kept going past the driveway and looked at the yard as he drove by. Leigh's car wasn't there. She always left it outside until just before dark. He saw that the grass was well past mowing. It was late April, and everyone was getting their lawn mowers out again.

Bill circled the block, and somehow his car steered itself into their driveway. He was off work early for a change. He could mow for Leigh and be gone before she got home. She usually worked later in the day than he did, probably more so now with her management job.

Bill got out of his car, punched in the house code, and opened the garage door. The lawn mower was just as he had left it last fall. He checked the oil but realized he would have to use the old gasoline.

To his relief, the mower started on the third pull. So Bill mowed his and Leigh's yard. It was small, so it didn't even take an hour. When he was done, he pushed the mower back into the garage and shut the door. He jumped into his car and headed to his apartment, hoping to miss Leigh coming down the street.

It wasn't long before Leigh pulled in and walked toward the house. She didn't see the cut grass at first - she smelled it. Leigh turned around from the front door and looked out across the yard. Big tears rolled down her cheeks when she saw the grass and knew he had been there, had cared for her.

Leigh bawled like a baby for several minutes when she went into the house. The first thing she did was text Bill a big thank-you.

Leigh went to her OBGYN the next day. It was time for the sonogram. She was over four months along now. She wanted to see pictures of the baby.

"We'll put ultrasound gel on your belly," said the nurse.

Next they moved the wand and looked at the screen. Leigh looked with joy as the image of a baby popped up on the screen, or at least what seemed to be one.

The nurse gave Leigh pictures of the sonogram's better exposures.

When the doctor came in, she commented on how well the pregnancy was going. "You're doing very well," she said. "Your weight gain is good but not too much."

Leigh stayed awake most of the night, thinking about how much she wanted to share this with Bill and what she could do for him, for helping her earlier that week.

I need something that won't make him mad, she thought. *There has to be something.*

Leigh didn't dare go back into his apartment without him being there. If she asked him to go to something public, people would recognize her. *I know Bill would hate that.* She decided to ask him to come for dinner again on Saturday. They could start earlier.

She called him, hoping he would answer.

"Hi, Bill," she said.

"Hello, Leigh," he answered. There was no animosity in his voice.

I hope he is glad to hear from me, she said to herself. "Bill, would you come for dinner on Saturday?" she asked.

Bill paused before he answered. Leigh crossed her fingers and toes.

"All right," he finally said. "What time do you want me to come?"

Leigh jumped with joy. "Would 5:00 p.m. be okay?" she said.

"Yes. I'll see you then."

Leigh thought Bill would like his typical meat and potatoes supper, so she planned for that. She also decided to take a risk and laid out her sonogram pictures on the cedar chest by the picture window.

Bill showed up a little before five and knocked on the front door again. Leigh opened it and greeted him with a smile. Bill came in, and they sat at the table.

"How was your week?" Leigh asked.

"It was good," he answered. "Same old same old. How is your new job at the station?"

"It's different but good," Leigh answered. "I don't know how Phil ever did all of those things by himself."

Leigh already had the table set. She brought out the simple meatloaf dinner, and they had their second meal together. Bill was obviously getting better toward her. She asked him about his living arrangements, as they finished supper.

"How is your new apartment?" she asked. "Are the neighbors good?"

Bill looked at her with one of his typical all-telling facial expressions. "I hate it," he answered. "The people in all of the other apartments are strange."

Leigh went on to talk about her job and navy reserve duties. "I like the management job," she said. "Navy is giving me time off. I don't have to drill until the baby is born."

Then Leigh asked Bill about his car.

"Is the old Ford running well?" she asked.

"Well, yes," he said. "I don't drive it that far. It doesn't look like much, but really it's sound, mechanically anyway."

He and Leigh visited for about a half an hour. Leigh didn't set out any desert. Then they got up and went into the living room. Bill saw the sonogram pictures laid out on the cedar chest. He didn't say a word, so Leigh spoke up.

"I don't know the sex yet," she said. "I think I want to wait."

Bill looked out the window, obviously not liking everything but not wanting to start up the why argument again. He looked at Leigh and then down at the sonogram pictures. He stared out the window for several seconds with no emotion showing on his face at all.

What happened next surprised Leigh more than anything her husband had ever done in their marriage. Still standing, he looked at Leigh, teared up, and then from out of nowhere, hit his wife. With his open right hand, the mild-mannered, balding short man struck Leigh so hard that he raised a welt across the side of her face and forehead.

Leigh didn't see the swing coming.

The sound scared Bill; he realized how hard he had hit her. She was the first woman he'd ever done that to in his life. She cried, he cried, and they both stood there looking at each other.

What happened next defied all logic and showed how close love and hate really were. It confirmed the truth in statements about strong, deep, and emotional love and want. Bill grabbed Leigh, and she grabbed back and they pulled each other into a longing embrace.

Next, the clothes flew off as they came together in an almost primal way. Bill and Leigh made love with a passion beyond anything they'd ever had before.

This was aggressive sex, rather than a patient and slow proceeding—an almost violent and prehistoric type of rut. The only coherent thing they managed was to make it into the bedroom, away from the picture window while it was still daylight.

Leigh was afraid to let go of Bill, afraid he might start thinking about what he was doing and change his mind. Bill wasn't about to change his mind.

Afterward, they lay in each other's arms for a long time, with Bill looking into Leigh's eyes. It was exactly where he wanted to be and what he wanted to do.

It was Leigh who spoke first. It was starting to get dark outside. "Are you hungry?" she asked. "I'm hungry."

"Yes," answered Bill. "I want something to drink."

They put on enough clothes to go back into the living room and kitchen. Leigh closed the drapes, and they sat at the table. Bill got out the ice water and wineglasses and opened a bottle of Cabernet. Leigh got out cheese, crackers, and the wrapped chocolate.

They sat and looked at each other as they ate. The side of Leigh's face and forehead was swollen and noticeably red from being hit. Her lips were puffy from the hard kissing, and she was sporting quite a sex hair display.

Bill didn't have much hair to mess up, but his thick chest hair was matted to his skin, still wet from their sweaty lovemaking.

The hitting another person topic should probably have been brought up, but they didn't. Bill felt bad about the welt and swelling he saw.

But Leigh didn't care. It wasn't that she thought she deserved it. She just wanted to be with her man, wanted him so badly that even she would let the domestic struggle go.

They had been sitting there for a while when Leigh finally spoke. "Stay with me," she said and asked at the same time. "Sleep in our bed tonight."

Bill didn't answer her. He looked at her but didn't want to seem easy on this in any way. He finished his wine and then got up to go to the bathroom.

Leigh put up the food, placed the dishes in the sink, and walked back through the living room. She began to silently cry, hoping with every ounce of her being that Bill would not leave. She looked around. Some of his clothes were still in the living room. None were in the bedroom as she walked in.

Leigh sat on the bed and listened to the bathroom door open. Then she heard the sound of him picking up his clothes. Leigh could tell he was standing there, probably thinking about what he was going to do. Then she heard him taking steps, not away but toward her.

He stepped inside the bedroom, put his clothes on a chair, and came toward the bed. Leigh lost it. She sobbed out loud as he sat beside her. Bill pulled her down onto the bed, and they lay alongside each other for a short second.

Round two of ferocious lovemaking began.

The next morning, Leigh didn't know what to do. She wanted her husband to stay. He had slept holding her, but now he was starting to wake. She rolled over to look at him, and he looked back into her eyes.

"Good morning, Mr. Andrews," Leigh said nervously. It was something she had said many times during their married years.

"Good morning to you, Mrs. Andrews," Bill replied.

Leigh sighed a silent breath. It felt so good to hear that.

They both got up. He went to shower, and she got her robe and went to the kitchen. Leigh made a pot of coffee and waited for Bill to come out of the bathroom. Bill found a clean towel on his old towel rack. His shaving kit was at his apartment, but he found the disposable razors in the drawer and used one of them.

He dressed in the same clothes, walked out into the kitchen, and sat in his chair at the table. Leigh brought him a cup of hot coffee, and they both sat at the table, looking at each other. Normally, they would have gotten ready for church. But not today. Leigh decided to try to say something.

"Would you like to do something today?" she asked.

Bill didn't answer. He simply sat like he really just wanted to be in his chair. "I don't know," he said. "I don't know what I want to do."

"Well, how about breakfast?" Leigh asked.

"Okay," he replied. "Sounds good."

Leigh cooked, and they had a good morning meal together. They talked about everything except the baby. Leigh wasn't about to mention a word on that subject. As Bill began to fidget a bit, Leigh knew she had better get to the hard stuff.

"Would you stay with me again?" she asked. Tears ran down both cheeks.

Bill didn't say anything and looked past Leigh to the wall behind her. "Leigh, I'll think about it," he said finally.

When Bill got up to go, Leigh offered to come with him, afraid that if she let him leave, he wouldn't come back.

"Let me go too," she said. "If you want to come back, I could help you get your stuff."

"I need to do that on my own," Bill calmly but sternly replied. "If I can do it, I'll be back."

Only because it made sense was Leigh able to let her man go out the door. But she insisted on walking to the car with him. Leigh looked at him through teary eyes, holding one of his arms, and asked one parting question.

"Can I kiss you good-bye?"

Bill was crying too. He turned to look her straight in the eye. He gave her a long good-bye kiss, made himself break it, and then got into his car.

Leigh watched him back out of the driveway and kept watching until his car was out of sight.

It was almost six thirty in the evening when Leigh looked out the window for the umpteenth time. She was so hoping he would come back. The sound of every car had made her look. But it was the sound of one that made her bolt out the door. The sound of Bill's old Ford was unmistakable, as it slowed for the driveway and pulled in.

Leigh ran along the walkway and then the driveway as he opened the door. She grabbed him before he had even gotten out of the car. Tears of joy, long pent-up frustration, and happiness all came to the surface.

Bill stood up with her hanging over him and hugged her back. With a carload of stuff, all he could get into the old Ford anyway, Leigh's husband, Bill, came back to her and was back in her life to stay.

The next morning at work, Leigh beamed with such happiness that coworkers noticed as soon as she walked through the door.

No one had to say a word. Her joy rubbed off on everyone. Secretaries she knew well cried tears of joy right with her. Phil came out of his office, took one look at Leigh, and gave her a big hug.

"Congratulations," he said. "I take it Bill came back?"

"Oh," was all Leigh could get out. With that, her coworkers almost applauded out loud.

Bill and Leigh waited until the next weekend to go get all of his furniture and move it back in. They borrowed the same trailer Leigh had used to take it over.

As the days passed, Bill was much happier. *I can forgive*, he had said to himself. Leigh noticed it too. She also noticed that Bill's moodiness had gotten much better. It was like he had matured and was older and wiser. He didn't let things bother him as quickly as he used to.

When the next OBGYN appointment came around, Leigh asked Bill if he would like to go. "We might do another sonogram," Leigh said. "Would you like to come see?"

"No," he said. "But you go ahead."

When Leigh came back home, she was very surprised at what she found. Bill was working on the baby's room. He had moved the furniture out and was busy getting the walls ready to paint.

Bill walked up and gave Leigh a big hug and kiss. "What color shall we paint this room?" he asked.

Leigh looked at him with tears in both eyes. "Blue," she said. "It's a boy!"

Over the next week, Bill did more work in the baby's room. He put up bands of wallpaper at the ceiling, middle of the wall, and baseboard. He even added a tall corner shelf.

"These are for the toys," he told Leigh. "Toy boxes are always dumped out, and shelves are easier to use."

Leigh watched him work but noticed that he never touched her baby bump, never commented on her looking pregnant, and never said a word about names.

He will be father to this baby, she said to herself. *I don't know that he is totally accepting this.*

Several weeks passed, and Leigh began to think about Kelly and the baby he would never know. She didn't want the baby to grow up like she had for much of her childhood, not knowing who her real father or stepsiblings were.

Leigh thought about her sister, Lynn. She wished they could have been friends when they were growing up. They could have talked about boys, school, and everything. Leigh also knew that Kelly's family would want to know about the baby and one day perhaps see and be a part of the baby's extended family.

I know they wouldn't want to right now, she said to herself. *People have to endure their adultery madness first.* Leigh also knew this would be breaking some new ground regarding affairs and illegitimacy. She didn't know how Bill would handle knowing Kelly's family. Confrontation was something he avoided like the plague.

Strange how my husband is so much like my grandmother, she thought. *In more ways than one. But there has to be a way, and I am going to try!*

She still worried desperately about Bill being able to handle fatherhood, as well as her ideas about the other family.

CHAPTER 18

After a few more days, she knew it was time to tackle it. She asked Bill to sit down and talk.

"Bill," she said. "I want to try to get you to understand something I have to do. Will you trust me on this one?"

"At the tone of your voice," he said, "I don't know if I do or not."

Leigh knew this probably wouldn't go well. "I want to go see Kelly's wife," she said. "I want to drive to Kansas, and I want you to take me."

Bill just looked at her in disbelief. "What in the hell!" he exclaimed. "Do you know what those people are going to think about you? If they don't know about the baby, just let them live the rest of their lives that way."

Leigh knew secrecy would be impossible, especially with social media.

"They will find out about the baby anyhow," she said. "Someone Kelly and I both knew will let the cat out of the bag, and when the baby gets older, he will want to know his other family. I am not going to let this baby grow up never knowing his real father, like I had to."

There was more to it, and Leigh wanted to go over it. "Bill, you've been around my stepsister Lynn. I will never get over missing out on the time I could have had with her!"

"Well, I say no," he said. "You are not going to upset Kelly's wife with this. She is probably worse off than you. Enough is enough!"

He walked out the door, got in his car, and left. Leigh didn't try to stop him. But she also knew this was something she was going to do, or eventually do, with or without him.

Bill came back later that evening. He didn't say a word.

This is back to his usual self, thought Leigh. *He did this before I went to Iraq.*

He didn't talk to her until the next day. He put his arms around her before he left for work. She hugged him back and didn't say a word.

It was four days before she brought it up again. She didn't have to say what she wanted to talk about.

"Bill," she said, "I want to go." That was all she said.

Bill didn't answer her, but he didn't storm out of the house either. This was how their fights had gone before. He would usually give in and let her do what she wanted, most of the time anyway.

The next Monday, she looked at him as he left for work. She didn't have to say anything. Bill looked back at her hard.

"How can you possibly think this is going to be a good thing?" he demanded.

"I get it over now," Leigh replied, "not later. And it may not be good for me, but it will be good, or become good, for the baby."

Leigh thought of something else that might help Bill to see. "Look into the future, Bill," she said. "Just try to see what will happen in the next five years."

Bill didn't say a word, like maybe he was trying to see the sense in this but just couldn't. Leigh decided to bring up the adoption word.

"Bill," Leigh said, "There will be an adoption process for us to go through, for you to become the legal father. I think I will have to notify Kelly's family for that. We will have to tell them anyway."

He thought for a few seconds before he spoke again, thinking that at least that statement made common sense. Bill looked Leigh straight in the eye.

"Are you going to drive by yourself if I don't go?" he asked.

"Right now, I just want you to accept that I want to do this. I don't want to drive by myself."

"Do I remember right that they live in Columbus, Kansas?" asked Bill.

"Yes," answered Leigh, knowing she had won the battle.

"I don't want to do this," he said. Then Bill went back to his present-tense thinking mode. "Do you realize you are starting to show?" With that he turned around and drove to work.

Leigh started making plans for Kansas. She would have to call Gwen.

On Monday evening, she called Kelly's home number. It was still in her cell phone.

"Hello," answered Gwen on the first ring.

"Hi, Gwen," said Leigh. "This is Leigh Andrews, Kelly's navy shipmate. I met you at a navy family gathering in 2005 in Norfolk."

"I remember you, Leigh," said Gwen, surprised that Leigh was back already from Iraq.

"Gwen," said Leigh. But she had to pause. "I would like to come see you and go to Kelly's grave."

Gwen was silent for a bit. It had been weeks since she had talked to any of Kelly's friends or family. "Well, you come right on," said Gwen. "I know you were a very close friend of Kelly's. When is a good time for you?"

"If we drive down this coming weekend, say get there on Saturday around noon, did you already have plans?"

"No plans at all," said Gwen, a little surprised that Leigh wanted to come that soon. "Be glad to have you come, and I want you to have lunch."

"I'd be glad to, Gwen," she said.

"I have stuff of Kelly's you could look at," she said. "He has pictures all over the house and even some of you saved on his computer. Can you bring a thumb drive to copy them?"

"Sure," said Leigh. "But I want to see you too," she said.

The women talked for a few minutes more and finished their arrangements.

On Monday evening, Bill asked Leigh if there was any talking her out of it. He could tell by her face there wasn't.

"I'll ask off of work for Friday," he said. "It's a fourteen-hour drive from Columbus to Columbus. We should stay in a motel in mid-Missouri somewhere, get up early, and drive the rest of the way."

"That's fine," said Leigh. "Gwen wants us to come in for lunch before we go to see Kelly's grave."

Bill just shook his head and walked out of the room. He couldn't believe Leigh wanted to do this, and that *he* was taking her!

On Friday morning at seven o'clock, they finished packing and left the house. They made it just past Saint Louis that evening and spent the night.

At six on Saturday morning, they proceeded southeast, and a little before noon, they rolled down Kelly and Gwen's driveway. Leigh had seen pictures of the farm and recognized the house. It was a beautiful summer day.

Gwen had rented the farm back to her brother-in-law. There were new dark green soybeans growing on three sides of the house. Planted in early May, the bean plants were almost a foot tall. The dirt between the rows showed dark brown.

Leigh got out of the car first, worried that Bill was going to melt into the floorboards. But he finally opened his door and followed her onto the porch.

Gwen met them at the door. Leigh was already crying. Gwen opened the front door and hugged Leigh. Both women stood there for almost a minute, quietly crying. Gwen broke the embrace and asked Leigh and Bill to sit down.

Bill was trying his best to show a brave face.

"How was your trip?" Gwen asked.

"Very good," said Bill.

They visited for several minutes before Gwen got up. "I've

got some homemade soup on the stove," she said. "Would you like some?"

"Sounds great," said Leigh. "Let me hit the h—bathroom before we sit down at the table."

"Did you start to say head?" asked Gwen. "I can tell you've been around Kelly for a while."

Bill swallowed hard.

"We all say that," said Leigh. "Navy just gets in your blood."

After a very nice lunch, the group headed out to the cemetery. Gwen walked beside Leigh to the grave. The VA had offered to provide a very nice gravestone, but Gwen had been encouraged by Jane to get a husband and wife one, with her name beside her husband's.

Kelly's name was on the left. His name, rank, and birth and death dates were listed. There was also a notation for his Navy Cross.

Leigh stood there looking with tears running down both cheeks. "It's beautiful, Gwen," she said.

"Kelly asked me to bury him here if anything happened. He was such a good man."

Now both women were bawling like babies.

They went back to the house, and Gwen's sister pulled into the driveway.

"I asked Jane to come meet you," said Gwen. "I hope that's okay."

"I would love to meet her," said Leigh. A feeling of apprehension washed over her, as she instinctively knew everything that was going on was about to come out.

Jane came into the house, and Bill and Leigh stood to shake hands. They talked for about an hour about the navy, TV station work, and Leigh's officer commission before Bill said they had a long way to go.

Leigh reached into her purse and got one of her navy cards out. It listed all of her contact numbers. She and Bill got up to leave. As Gwen stood, Leigh walked over and hugged her again. Both women cried for several seconds. Then Leigh turned and hugged Jane. She put her card into Jane's hand as she turned to go.

Leigh and Jane looked at each other for a long second. Then Bill opened the door, and they headed for the car and the first leg of their trip back to Ohio.

Jane kept standing as Gwen sat back down on the couch. As Bill and Leigh's car backed out of the driveway and drove away, Jane looked at Gwen hard.

"What's wrong?" asked Gwen.

After waiting a few seconds before answering, Jane responded, "She's pregnant!"

Bill and Leigh hadn't driven very far when he broke the silence. "Leigh, what are you doing?"

Leigh thought for a few seconds before she answered. "Bill, I'm not sure you will understand, and I hope you will trust me on this one. I want to get the truth about this baby over with now, not months or years down the road. I've prayed about it and talked with Pastor Evans, and this is what God is leading me to do. Try for a second to think about what is good for the baby, not me or us or even Gwen."

Bill wasn't impressed at all with the religious or baby talk. "I think Jane figured out you were pregnant," he said. "And I saw you give her your card."

"I know she did," said Leigh. "I hope she will call me."

"Do you realize what this will do to Gwen?" he said.

"Bill, when do I want to do it? When is it a good time?"

Bill didn't answer. Leigh really thought she was right. Time would tell if things would work out.

Jane looked at Gwen, waiting for the "she's pregnant" statement to hit her. She saw Gwen's eyes open wide. Her sister was unable to say anything for several seconds.

"No," Gwen said, "not Kelly, and I can't believe Leigh would."

"I think they did, Gwen," said Jane. "Why else would she be back early?"

"Kelly went away with Leigh on trips for years," said Jane. "I would know it if they were having an affair, if he was having an affair."

"Well, they probably weren't having one then," said Jane. "But I think they did now. Or rather when they were in Iraq, they did, obviously."

"I don't want to have something else happen to me, not again," said Gwen. She was standing now, holding her hands over her mouth. "Why do you think it was Kelly?" she asked. "There are any number of men who could be the father. How do you know she was pregnant anyway?"

"Gwen, the woman is obviously pregnant. She's showing. I could tell as soon as she stood up. And the way she looked at me when she gave me her card. I think she wanted me to know!"

Gwen stood and didn't say anything for several seconds. "I want to know that it's Kelly's," she said. "I'm not going to believe this until I know."

Jane didn't know what she should do at first. Her sister couldn't, or wouldn't, see it.

Gosh, how can married women be so naïve? she thought as she drove the short distance back to her and David's farm. Her minister's wife marriage counseling experience was coming into play.

Jane really didn't want to get involved in this. And why should Gwen be involved at all? She hadn't cheated on anyone. She was just getting back on her feet following Kelly's death.

"Ugh," said Jane to herself. "I would so unload on Kelly if I could. How could this man do something like this? And to Gwen?"

Jane thought about it through Saturday evening and Sunday all through church. If Kelly had fathered another child, Gwen would want to know and would want to know things about the baby.

She made her decision to call Leigh.

Leigh and Bill made it home by early Sunday evening. Leigh thought the whole way home about Gwen and what she and Jane were going through.

She looked at the phone, wondering if it would ring. It wasn't long before the home phone broke the silence.

"Hello," said a very nervous Leigh, recognizing the 620 Kansas area code on the caller ID.

"Hello, this is Jane, Gwen's sister. Is this Leigh?"

"Yes, Jane. I've been trying to prepare for if you called."

Jane waited a second and then started in with what she wanted to say. Her mother-in-law from hell abilities went from first to high gear in an instant.

"What are you trying to accomplish here? How is any of this good for Gwen or you?"

Leigh took a deep breath and made her reply. "Jane, I'm pregnant from an affair with Kelly. Everyone involved will know or figure that out in time. I want to come forward now!"

Jane didn't wait very long before answering back in force.

"Then fine. You did it. Kelly did it. But it's over. Have the baby or an abortion or whatever. But leave Gwen out of it. Do you realize what she is going through right now?"

Leigh was crying now. The impact of her decision came full force. She didn't answer Jane.

"Leigh, I work as a minister's wife and deal with marriages affected by affairs. I know what they do to them and to the families."

This time Leigh was able to respond. "Don't blame Kelly," she said. "Blame me! And I'm not having an abortion, Jane. I am having and keeping this baby. I mean that!"

Jane paused for a bit, having been corrected, and rightly so.

"Leigh, I'm glad you're having the baby. I shouldn't have said what I did about abortion. But couldn't you just have had the baby and Gwen never know? Wouldn't that be better for everyone involved?"

Leigh was smart. She would become a good naval officer and leader. She knew Jane and Bill were not seeing what would happen down the road.

"Jane," said Leigh, "I gave you my card because I thought you could be someone who could help with this, with all that is going to happen. I want to ask you something. I've told you that Kelly is the father. Would you think on what we've said today? Then someday, if anyone wanted to, we could talk again?"

"No," said Jane. "That would only make things worse. Stay out of Gwen's life, Leigh!"

"Could we go for now," said Leigh, "and just think this over for the time being?"

Jane really didn't know what to say now. But ending the conversation seemed to be the right thing. "Well, I'm ready to go then," she said, raising her arm in resolution. "Good-bye."

"Good-bye," said Leigh, shaking all over from the tension of the moment.

Jane decided not to wait with this news and felt she should go see Gwen now. Gwen had asked her to find out for sure if her husband had cheated.

Jane was used to being a minister's wife. She had dealt with affairs, drug abuse, suicide, and everything that comes with being God's place for church members to ask for help. This was like those situations, but it went further. When affairs became public, people divorced, kids suffered, and life went on.

With this, Kelly was dead, his war-hero image was tarnished, and the widow and her angry sister had no one to take it out on except for the pregnant hussy.

Jane's minister husband, David, had listened to the conversation.

"Can you believe this?" Jane said as she looked at him.

"This is the first time I've ever had someone come and say they had an affair and were pregnant from it," David said. "This girl has some set of balls!"

Jane couldn't believe her husband had said that. "What are you," she asked, "proud of her?"

"On no," David replied. "I couldn't feel worse for Gwen. And there will be more to come, Jane."

She didn't know what her husband meant by that, but she dreaded what she had to tell her sister. *Oh*, thought Jane. *How come I have to be the one to bring all of the bad news to Gwen?* She thought seriously about having Laura do it. But Laura was still a grown kid, the same age as her own daughter. *No*, she said to herself. *I will do this myself.*

It was just after eight on Sunday evening when Jane drove to Gwen's house. Gwen saw her van as it pulled up the driveway. She wondered if Jane had called Leigh.

Gwen opened the door as Jane walked onto the porch. Jane swallowed hard and went into the living room. No one said anything for a few seconds. Both women were still standing.

"Did you call her?" said Gwen.

Jane looked at her sister. "Yes, I did," she said. "Gwen, brace yourself."

With that, Gwen started to cry. "No. Kelly wouldn't do that."

"Gwen, affairs happen. You don't even realize how many people you personally know have had them, and don't ask who, because I won't tell you."

Gwen knew that Jane counseled many churchgoers with David. She was probably right that much more of this went on than folks realized. She looked at Jane and just shook her head.

"It was a war, Gwen," said Jane. "Sometimes people think it is all right to do things in that situation, when they wouldn't otherwise."

Gwen wasn't saying anything, just listening and trying to believe that this had really happened. Then she said something Jane didn't expect to hear.

"What about the baby? Kelly *is* the father."

Jane looked at her sister hard. "You missed something," she said. "You're supposed to be mad at Kelly right now."

"I am mad at Kelly," she said. "I was mad all night. And when I get to heaven he is going to get it from me big time. But what is going to happen to this baby?"

The next week, Bill called from his work phone and asked their pastor to meet with him.

"Do you want Leigh to come?" the pastor asked.

"No," said Bill. "I want to come by myself."

He stopped by early on a Saturday morning. He had told Leigh he was just going to the store.

"How's it going?" asked the pastor.

"Not well," Bill said. "I'm not sure I can do all of this, all that Leigh is wanting to do."

"What's that?" asked the pastor.

"Leigh made me go with her to see the dead man's wife and family," Bill said. "I just don't see the sense in any of this!"

The preacher thought for a bit before he spoke again. "What did she tell you? Why did she want to go?"

"She said she wanted Kelly's family to know about the baby."

"Anything else?"

Bill went on to describe that Leigh had grown up without knowing her father, and that she had stepbrothers and stepsisters she hadn't gotten to know or grow up with. She hadn't been allowed to be around them at all until after she was grown.

The pastor thought again. "Well, you don't have to do this," he said. "I can tell you don't want to see these people."

"No, I don't," Bill said. "I don't know if I can stay with Leigh if this is what she wants to do."

The pastor waited for a moment and then spoke to Bill slowly and deliberately. "Can I suggest you try something?" he said. "Take a Post-it note, write what you are thinking about doing, and stick it to your mirror when you get home from work. The next morning as you get ready for work, you can decide if you still want to do what that note says."

Bill thought about the idea.

"I can do that," he said. "We get ready in different bathrooms. But I don't want to write down what I'm thinking on the note. I can just put up a blank one."

The pastor smiled inwardly. He had advised this many times in marriage counseling. If one partner or the other actually wrote on the note, he or she was beyond serious. Bill was obviously not, and the pastor was glad for it, for both Leigh and Bill.

Bill went home and did the note thing every night. And every morning he took the Post-it down. He didn't want to do what Leigh was doing, but he didn't want to leave her over it. Bill loved his wife, in spite of the affair, the baby, and her wild ideas about knowing this other family.

CHAPTER 19

Leigh went back to work, and several months went by. She was really showing now. Her fellow TV station employees were as good to her as she could have ever asked.

They would help her carry anything, and always asked her to lunch if they went out.

When the fall rains began to come, coworkers made sure she had a parking space close to the back door. They always offered to walk her to her car if she stayed late in the evening.

If anyone was still strange, it was Bill. He had always wanted a baby. He and Leigh had talked about it for years, especially in the early years of their marriage.

But he was not his former self.

I've got the affair to blame, Leigh thought. *And there is no one more at fault than me.* She knew she would have to live with her infidelity for the rest of her life.

Bill looked at his bright yellow Post-it note every morning. *No, I don't want to leave*, he would tell himself. But Bill didn't quite know what he did want to do.

Growing up, he had wanted to be an athlete, like the jocks he had always been so jealous of. He had tried out for baseball and track. But he spent all his time sitting on the bench and coming in last in every event. He just wasn't strong or athletic. Leigh was the main thing he was proud of. He had been proud to walk into rooms with her. She was so pretty and outgoing and attracted all of the attention he had never received.

And Bill didn't quite know what he was going to do with a baby. He was glad it was a boy, but he had no idea how he was going to be a father.

Leigh had mentioned picking out names. But he always stopped talking when she brought it up.

At least he won't grow up to be like me, Bill thought. Kelly had been tall and athletic. And Leigh was very athletic herself, though certainly not big and tall.

Growing up, Bill's peer idol had been his cousin Beau, the star baseball pitcher from his family. Bill's uncle had even given him a glove and encouraged him to play baseball too. One day, Bill took the old glove out of his closet. He looked into the baby's room, and his first dad thought came into his head. *I can teach him to play catch one day*, thought Bill. *That's what I can do!*

Bill walked back to their bedroom and made the mistake of setting his glove down on their dresser. He made the mistake of leaving it there, when he went to the store.

That night, Leigh came into the bedroom and saw the baseball glove. She had walked past it at first, and then her eyes had opened wide as she realized what she had seen.

Leigh whirled around, exclaiming out loud when she saw the glove again. All of her pent-up anxiety came to the surface and she cried aloud.

As Bill came out of his bathroom and into their bedroom, Leigh ran to him.

"Well, what's gotten into you?" Bill exclaimed.

They were embracing by the dresser, and Leigh reached out and picked up the glove.

"I forgot to put that back," Bill said.

Leigh was able to get past her tears and looked him square in the eye. "You got this out for our baby boy," she blurted and then started bawling again.

"Well, lie down on the bed for bit," Bill replied. "I guess I did get it out for him."

Leigh and Bill lay down, and she put her head on his chest, still holding on to the baseball glove. She finally spoke. "Are you ready to talk about names yet?" she asked.

Bill didn't say anything for a bit and just looked at Leigh and the glove she was still holding. Leigh spoke again about the baby's name.

"You could pick it out, you know," Leigh said. "Isn't there something that would sound good to you?"

Bill didn't reply at first but finally said what was on his mind. "Maybe one," he finally said. "But you might not like it."

"Try me," she demanded.

"Well … Beau," Bill blurted. He paused for a bit before he said something else. "I knew you wouldn't like it."

Leigh looked at him with twinkling eyes. "I just happen to know a Beau from your family," she said. "The baseball pitcher cousin who got a tryout with the Cincinnati Reds!"

Bill grinned when she said that. It was obvious that he was very proud of this relative.

Leigh spoke again. "I like it," she said. "Beau is very good name, and I think both of them would be very proud to share it."

When October rolled around, Leigh knew it was about time to deliver. She told Bill it was close.

He was getting better and being more helpful with baby preparations. He had painted a big baseball on one wall of the baby's room. He even went with Leigh to buy furniture.

Leigh still worried about him accepting the baby. She honestly didn't know for sure if he would. But she prayed that God would help with that part. Much as she loved Bill, she would leave him if necessary to raise the coming child.

Her pastor, who had also been functioning as a marriage counselor, had told her to give Bill things he wanted from a marriage. He also said to make sure she was letting Bill know what she wanted too. While it was her idea to have him name the baby, Leigh felt she should do more to make sure that Bill felt like he was as much a part of their marriage and the baby rearing as he wanted to be.

When they brought the baby home, she would have to do more to make Bill a big part of the child rearing, teaching, and parental love sharing.

Late one afternoon, she was standing in the kitchen. She had just come in from the TV station. She felt something warm. Her water was breaking. Bill was still on his way home when she called.

"What's up, babe?" he said as he answered his phone.

"I think my water broke," she said.

"I'll be right there," he said without thinking. Bill quickly sped up and began passing cars on the freeway.

Leigh had cleaned up the mess in the kitchen and was changing clothes when Bill slid into the driveway. They were gone from the house in one minute.

They got to the hospital before six in the evening. The emergency room front desk recognized that Leigh was in labor and hurried her through the hospital sign-in procedure. Soon Leigh was in a delivery room and counting minutes between contractions. Her OBGYN arrived and began measuring dilation. Leigh was in excellent physical condition, and her labor was going very well.

Almost seven hours later, she delivered a healthy eight-pound, fifteen-ounce boy. He was twenty-two inches long.

The nurses brought the baby over to Mom to hold for the first time. Leigh and Bill both bawled like babies as Leigh took him into her arms. She just beamed with smiles and tears. Bill did too. She was exhausted when the nurses came in to complete the baby's exam. She looked up and saw Bill quietly crying. He looked at Leigh and then at the baby.

"Hey there, Dad," said Leigh. "You doing all right?"

"Yes," he answered, "just worried about you. I've never seen you strain so hard."

Leigh reached out and held his hand.

"You are the happiest I've ever seen you!" Bill said.

The nurses took Leigh to her room, and soon they brought in

the baby. He was wrapped in a bright white blanket and wore a baby blue gown. One of the attending nurses spoke to Leigh.

"What are we going to name this baby?" she asked.

Leigh looked at Bill for his approval. "Beau," she said. "Beau William."

Later on when the nurse brought in the birth certificate, Leigh listed the parents' names in the proper places. She put herself as the mother and Kelly Raines as the father, and in parentheses she put Bill as the adoptive father.

I don't know if that is legal, she thought. *But I'm doing it.*

Bill watched as Leigh filled out the birth certificate and noticed that Beau's last name was Raines. Leigh was watching for that.

"Are you okay with that, Pop?" she asked.

Bill didn't say anything for a minute, but then he nodded and smiled at Leigh.

"We will change that when we go through the adoption," Leigh said. "It will just be Raines for now."

The nurse helping with the paperwork didn't say a word.

Later that afternoon, the nurse working with the birth certificate came back by Leigh's room. She had been waiting for Bill to leave.

"Mrs. Andrews," she said. "May I talk to you for a minute?"

"Yes," said Leigh as she looked up at the tall nurse.

"I want to say something about your adoption listing. I want to encourage you to see a lawyer and get all of the paperwork and court proceedings completed for your husband to become the adoptive parent. Your lawyer will send documents to the real father too. It gives him the opportunity to contest if he wants to. I want to warn you about that."

"He won't," said Leigh. "He died in Iraq."

The nurse looked at Leigh for a few seconds as she figured everything out. "You may still have to send notification to the other family," she said. "I hope everything works out for you and the baby." With that, she walked out the door.

I knew we would have to notify Kelly's family about adoption! Leigh exclaimed to herself. *I am so glad that part of my affair revelation is behind us!*

Leigh also knew she would have to work Bill through another thing now, but she thought he would accept the adoption process.

Bill went to work the next day, and Leigh and the baby stayed in the hospital. The nursery brought the baby to Leigh several times throughout the day to breastfeed. Leigh just beamed every time they brought him in.

He looks just like Kelly, she thought, *with his broad face, long legs, and big shoulders. He doesn't look anything like Bill.* And he had Leigh's light complexion and hair. Bill had a dark complexion and was bald with average height. *I hope no one picks up on that,* she thought. But babies' appearances could change quite a bit from when they were first born. When their hair was combed and they were wrapped in clothing and blankets, their looks could be quite different.

Bill came straight to the hospital after work. Leigh's thoughts about resemblance were as prophetic as could be.

"He looks just like Kelly," said Bill as the nurse brought the baby in for feeding time. "And maybe a little like you too," he added. Bill's tone seemed accepting of the strong resemblance to real dad Kelly, and of the baby not looking anything like him.

Leigh just rolled her eyes. "He looks like a baby," she said. "He doesn't look very much like anybody."

Bill looked at his wife for a second. "He and you are as beautiful as can be," he said. "All I could think about all day was seeing you with our new baby boy."

CHAPTER 20

As the months went by, Gwen had wondered about the baby too. Jane had told her how Leigh insisted that there would be no abortion, that she was having and keeping the baby. Mad as Gwen was and as hurt as she was by the affair, she loved Kelly more.

Oh, if he had lived, things might be quite intense, she thought. She hadn't spoken to Leigh since. The social interaction they'd had was something Gwen could not do, maybe never do.

But every day she thought about the baby. This was part of Kelly, and this was something else from him that she loved, or wanted to love.

Jane didn't quite know how to help Gwen with this. She was so curious about the coming baby.

You know, Jane thought, *this baby will be illegitimate*. In the past, the baby would have been hidden and shunned. But this was going on the year 2006, and times had changed. Illegitimate children were much more accepted now. And for sure, most families had them in their past.

Gwen had asked Jane to call Leigh for several days now. Had it been delivered, and if everything was all right, were some of the big questions Gwen had.

This is the strangest thing I've ever seen, Jane thought. The couples she helped David counsel with infidelity just divorced and stayed mad. *This one is so different. And how did it end up that I'm the go-between? I really don't like doing this.*

Jane had a lot of hurt from her sister's loss too. She didn't want to be part of all the drama involving this illegitimate baby, Kelly's affair, and the huge disruptions to her life.

Jane thought about it again and decided to make a decision. *Enough is enough*, she said to herself. *I am ending this now.*

Instead of calling Leigh, Jane went to see Gwen. She drove the half mile to her sister's house and walked to the door. Gwen heard the van and was already walking outside as Jane got out.

"Gwen, I'm done with this!" Jane said. "We are not going any further with this baby thing. It's over."

Gwen was surprised to see her sister this emphatic, but she was. Gwen just stood there.

"I want you to get busy with your own son and daughter," Jane said. "Move on from Kelly. Let the affair go."

Gwen was able to speak this time. "I don't want to think about the affair or Kelly," she said. "I just want to know about the baby."

Jane's response came quickly. "Well, I don't want to know about the baby or Leigh or Kelly or any of it!"

Jane didn't come in the house. But she didn't want to just tell her sister off and drive away. "Gwen," she said, "I'm going into town to shop for a while. Do you want to go?"

Gwen said yes and grabbed her purse.

But the shopping trip was horrendously quiet. Gwen didn't want to talk much about anything Jane brought up.

I just want to know about the baby, Gwen said to herself as they drove home.

At church on Sunday, David spoke to Gwen outside after the service. Jane was still inside the sanctuary.

"How's it goin'?" asked David. "You look a little down today."

Gwen looked back at the minister. "Jane doesn't want me to find out about the baby. She's really tired of being involved."

David thought for a minute before he answered. "I don't have the hardest job in the church," he answered. "She does. Most people don't see that."

Gwen had seen it before, but she hadn't thought about it lately.

David continued, "Let me talk to her. We had some really hard drama to deal with a few months ago. I had to help with a family molestation case, and Jane got drug in too. It was really bad."

Gwen remembered the family. They had been to church a few times.

"Maybe Jane is right," Gwen said. "Perhaps I should forget about Kelly's baby."

"No you don't," David said. "God put me and Jane here for things like this. Let me talk to her."

Gwen said good-bye to her pastor and headed home.

As David and Jane drove to their farm, David brought up Gwen.

"Gwen didn't look real good today," he said.

"I know," Jane answered. "She wants to learn about this baby, and I don't want to do it."

"Well, you don't have to do it," David answered. "Maybe I could step in and help some."

Taking turns with a task they shouldn't have to do, didn't sit well with Jane at all.

"Neither one of us should have to help," Jane answered. "Why can't this Ohio girl just go away?"

David sat quietly for a bit. "Well, she didn't Jane. I think Gwen really wants to do this."

Jane began to feel like she was listening to David's sermon, instead of talking to her husband. "You sound like Elijah the prophet now," she reminded him.

"I wasn't trying to," David answered, smiling inwardly, knowing full well that God was putting pressure on Jane's heart, just like he had for David countless times.

The rest of the ride home was quiet.

Later that afternoon, Jane began to think to herself. *Gwen can't make herself talk to Leigh. If it weren't for the baby, Gwen never would.* With that, Jane, the minister's wife, the churches "volun'told by God family counselor," made herself get up and walk to the phone in their office. She dialed Leigh's number, and it began to ring.

"Hello," said Leigh when she recognized Jane's number.

"Hello, Leigh," Jane said. "I guess I'm ready to call you back."

Leigh didn't know what to make of Jane's tone, but she was happy she had reached out.

"I'm glad you called," Leigh said. "I was hoping you would."

"Gwen really wants to know about this baby," Jane said with exasperation, "and I'm calling for her."

Leigh sighed with relief at finally hearing that. It was what she wanted to hear, both for the baby and for what might take place in the future.

"It's a baby boy," said Leigh. "He weighed almost nine pounds and was twenty-two inches long. He has my hair and complexion, but he looks like Kelly," she said. "He looks a lot like Kelly."

Jane didn't plan on tears being part of her conversation. She went from mad that she had to do something, to being caught up in the emotion. She had to pause for a second.

Leigh hadn't planned on hearing her tears through the phone, but there they there. She waited for Jane to speak.

"Well, I'm glad for the baby and for you, Leigh. You are obviously a very good mother. I'm not sure what the future is going to bring for Gwen, but I know she will want to hear all of this."

"Jane, I want to e-mail you pictures. Will you let me do that?"

"Yes," said Jane.

The two women exchanged e-mail addresses and established the fact that Jane could call again in the future to learn more about the baby.

"I forgot to ask one thing," said Jane. "What did you name him?"

"It's Beau," said Leigh. "Beau William Raines."

After the phone call, Jane waited a few minutes before she called Gwen.

No, thought Jane. *I better go down there for this.*

Gwen heard the car pulling into the driveway. She looked out the window to see Jane's van.

Jane walked into the house and stood looking at Gwen.

"Did you call?" asked Gwen.

"Yes," said Jane. "It's a boy."

Gwen's eyes widened, and her expression was one of amazement and even joy.

"Is he all right?" she asked.

"He's as healthy as can be," Jane said. She went on to give Gwen the weight, length, and other particulars. "I should have pictures on my e-mail," she said. "Let's go to your computer to bring them up."

Gwen led Jane to Kelly's old office and writing desk. Jane brought up her account and clicked on Leigh's e-mail attachments. The program was a little slow as Kelly's Photoshop program took over to display the shots.

The baby boy popped up on the screen. Jane and Gwen looked at him for almost a minute in silence. He didn't just look like Kelly; he was Kelly. Gwen started to cry first, and that started Jane going. The sisters stayed that way for a long minute.

Finally, Jane brought up the other pictures.

"I've never seen a baby resemble a father so much," said Gwen.

Then a thought hit Gwen like a freight train. Jane could tell something big had happened.

"I wish he was mine," Gwen said. "Oh, how I wish this baby was mine!"

Jane hadn't prepared herself for this. If she had known this would happen, she wouldn't have come. "Hey there, sis," she said. "We don't have to look at these any more. Let's just sit and talk."

Gwen held her hands over her face and sobbed for a few seconds, glancing at the computer screen. Jane shut it off and led her sister to the living room to sit down.

"You just take a minute," Jane said. "Let's sit for a while."

Jane had expected this to be something Gwen wanted and would like. The jealousy had blindsided her completely. Gwen stopped crying and looked out the window.

"I could just kick that man," she said. "How could he have an affair and father a child with another woman?" She shook her head.

Jane waited a few seconds before responding. "Gwen," she said. "I remember a sister who flatly stated that she didn't want any more children. A sister who had a benign tumor hysterectomy in part to prevent any accidental pregnancies."

If it had been anyone else, Gwen wouldn't have let him or her say those words.

"I didn't want any more kids," she said. "But that was before Kelly died. If I can't have him … Oh, I just wish the baby were mine. And I wish he wasn't Leigh's."

"Gwen, you haven't asked any more questions yet."

Gwen looked at Jane hard. "Did she name him Kelly?" she asked.

"No," said Jane. "It's Beau, but his last name is Raines."

Gwen just looked at Jane when she said the last name. "She really did that? It's not Andrews?"

Jane explained that she didn't know if a mother had to name a baby after his or her real father but that Leigh had done so. She also said that Leigh's husband, since he was still there, would probably adopt the boy and that they would probably change the last name to Andrews then.

Jane and Gwen talked for almost an hour about how she missed her husband and now this other woman had a baby who looked so much like him. Jane just listened patiently and then left.

I think I should just let Gwen deal with this for a while, Jane thought.

CHAPTER 21

The months passed, and Leigh watched her little boy grow from a crawler into a toddler. He walked at exactly one year. As he grew, he looked more and more like his real dad, Kelly. As much as that was happening, no one could tell it by Bill. He became the perfect father.

They had gone to a lawyer to formalize the adoption. Everything went through without a hitch. They included the process to change Beau's last name from Raines to Andrews.

Leigh watched as Bill looked at his last name going behind Beau's onto the official document. This was something Bill wanted, and Leigh was going to do it for him, and for Beau.

It's got to be easier for a child to have the same last name as their parents, she thought.

Leigh had notified Jane of what she was doing and of the name change. Leigh's counsel wanted to give Gwen the chance to challenge custody if she wanted to. Jane had thought about that and decided she wasn't going to let Gwen do that. She would insist as a sister, that Gwen not do that. Jane told Leigh that there would be no contest from Gwen and that she doubted there would be conflicts from any of Kelly's family.

One thing Jane did do was to get a legal opinion herself. A local lawyer had advised her that no judge would keep Bill from becoming the adoptive father.

"Does Gwen want to try to obtain custody or visitation rights?" he had asked. "Because I would advise against trying to do anything." He went on to say that if the current parents were good, there just wasn't a strong case. He also encouraged Jane to notify Kelly's family of the presence of the child. "This will give anyone wanting to challenge custody the opportunity to do so. If they choose not to, then it is their decision to live with."

Jane told Gwen of her attorney's legal opinion first. Thankfully, Gwen hadn't asked about challenging anything.

After explaining to Gwen that this was the best thing, Jane had called all of Kelly's kids and graciously explained that they had a stepbrother and about the adoption. Gwen's kids already knew.

While all of Kelly's kids had been shocked to learn the news, they all seemed to handle it without any big emotional fits.

As time passed, curiosity rather than anger and disgust began to grow from the Raines family. Everyone, from Gwen to the grown kids to Jane, wanted to know about baby Beau. And they all wanted to see the latest pictures.

Jane e-mailed Leigh and asked if she could send more shots. Leigh agreed, and the hottest e-mail item for months between Gwen and all of the kids were the newest pictures of baby Beau.

Soon young Beau was two years old, getting into everything, and beginning to talk. His hair had changed from reddish blond to white blond. His eyes were bright blue, not Leigh's pale blue or Kelly's hazel. Leigh and Bill didn't know how much the baby resembled Kelly's son, Josh, or Josh's son, JJ, who had been born just after Kelly's death.

Leigh and Bill worked with Beau constantly to read children's books, play, complete puzzles, and give him their every attention.

Pictures of Beau were the talk of Gwen and Jane's families.

As Beau turned from three to four years old, Leigh decided it was time to tell her son about his real father. She dreaded having to work Bill through it, but it wouldn't be right if she didn't tell him first.

Bill was getting dressed when she walked into their bedroom.

"Bill, I want to tell Beau about his biological dad. It's time."

Her husband gave her his typical clam-up response.

"We've got to do this sooner or later," she said.

"Well, you're going to do what you want to do," said her husband in his typical bad-mood response.

"I want you to understand," Leigh said.

"Leigh, just do it then. Maybe now is the right time," Bill said as he headed outside for his old grouch walk.

Leigh got her picture album and walked to Beau's room. "Hey guy," she said. "I need to talk to you."

Beau walked over to his mom, and she pulled him up onto her lap.

"Do you know who this is?" said Leigh as she opened the album to a picture of Kelly.

"I've seen his picture before. I know his name is Kelly. I've heard you talk about him getting killed in the war."

Leigh swallowed hard and began to speak. "Beau, this is your real dad. Bill is your dad too. But Kelly Raines is your natural father. We changed your last name from Raines to Andrews when dad Bill adopted you."

"How can I have two dads?" asked Beau.

"In Iraq, your mom did a very bad thing. I had a relationship with your real dad, Kelly, who wasn't my husband. I got pregnant with you from that relationship."

"Why didn't you get pregnant from Dad?" he asked.

"Well, there were medical problems with both dad Bill and I, and it just never happened. But it happened with Kelly while I was in the war, before he was killed in action."

Beau looked at the picture with fascination. Leigh was glad he wasn't upset about this, at least not so far. Then he said something that just knocked her socks off. Beau looked his mom right in the eye. "You better not do that again, Mom."

Leigh looked at him with wide eyes. "Well, I won't," she said. She picked him up and hugged him hard.

She didn't say that if she did, dad Bill wouldn't take her back again.

Gwen was also keeping track of Beau's fourth birthday.

She showed up at Jane's house and said something that totally blew her sister away.

"Jane, I would like to see Beau," she said. "I want you to help figure out a way for me to do that."

Jane looked at her sister hard for a second. "Gwen, are you sure about this?"

"Yes," she said. "I've seen enough pictures, and its time. Do you think Leigh would do that?"

"I don't know," said Jane. "But let me do something about it, probably just call her and ask."

"You want to what?" asked an astounded Bill.

He had just come home from work like he always did. As a husband, he didn't really ask a lot from his wife. If Leigh cooked supper and was someone for him to talk to and make love to, he was as happy as he could be. He was a simple and good man in every way. He hadn't expected to hear what his wife wanted them to do.

"Bill, I want to take Beau to see his other family. Jane called me earlier today, and Gwen has asked to see him and for Kelly's kids to see him."

Bill shook his head at the thought of seeing all these people and of even being there.

"Jane asked if Beau knew about his real dad," Leigh said. "I told them we already had that talk."

Bill wasn't having any of this, especially when it came to going to southeast Kansas again.

"I went to that house when you were pregnant," he said. "I don't want to do that again. No."

"Bill, you're the adoptive father. I can't take him there without your permission."

"Leigh, I don't want to go. I don't. Do you realize how hard it was to sit there last time? I almost didn't go then, and I thought seriously about leaving you on the spot."

Leigh paused when she heard those hurtful words. But she was used to Bill. He wouldn't understand this, and she wasn't about to try to make him.

She answered in her quiet way. "I want to go, Bill. Will you let me? Will you let Beau? I don't want him to grow up like me, never knowing his real father or his other family."

Bill didn't say anything for a few seconds. Then he grabbed his jacket and headed for the door. He paused at the doorway.

"I'm not leaving," he said. "I just want to walk and think awhile."

Leigh was glad for his comments. In the middle of a fight it was good to hear the other person say something like that.

Bill came back about an hour later and didn't say anything. They went to bed that night with him in a typical mood of not wanting Leigh to do what she was going to do.

The next morning as they dressed for work, Leigh looked at Bill for a second.

"Leigh," he said. "I'm not going with you this time. I don't want to endure what I had to last time. I won't say you can't take Beau. But I am *not* going!"

Leigh didn't say anything and just accepted his decision.

One day after getting Bill's reluctant okay, Leigh called Jane to plan for the meeting. It would be in two weeks. Jane instructed Leigh to speak to Gwen, but no more unless Gwen was able to comfortably engage in a conversation.

"I can't tell you Gwen is ready," said Jane. "I want you to take this very slowly and not to expect her to accept you."

"I'm fine with that," said Leigh. "I will watch for her body language and answer only what she asks me."

On the day of the trip, Bill spoke to his wife as he left for work.

"You're all set to go," he said. "The SUV is all serviced—tires aired up and fluids topped off."

"Thank you, dear," said Leigh.

"I still don't want to go," Bill said. "But maybe if this happens again, I will come."

Leigh breathed a big sigh of relief.

"I'm glad to hear that," she said.

EPILOGUE

At ten o'clock on a fall Saturday morning, Leigh pulled her SUV into Columbus, Kansas. She could see the nearby typical midwestern town park. The blue swimming pool was on one end, closed now for the season. Tall brown swings, wooden shingled picnic shelters, and horseshoe pits were on the other.

Jane and Gwen were already there in one of the shelter houses. Both of Kelly's grown kids had arrived, along with Gwen's daughter, Laura. Gwen's son, John, was the only one who didn't attend.

"John thinks there might be some drama," Laura had told her mother Gwen. "He thinks he had enough of that dealing with Dad during the divorce."

Leigh took a deep breath and got out of the car. She unbuckled Beau from his car seat, and together they walked toward the group by the picnic shelter. She tried her best not to cry.

Then Gwen's eyes met Leigh's, and both women started streaming tears. Beau didn't pick up on what was going on, and most eyes were on him. He looked like a carbon copy of Josh's son, JJ. All of Kelly's family noticed that.

Leigh walked Beau right up to Gwen. Leigh was shaking all over. Beau stood there, looking around and taking everything in.

Jane was very nervous about how this would go and so concerned for Gwen. She and David had prayed for days that everything would go well.

Gwen spoke first. "Hi there, Beau!"

Leigh gave another big sigh of relief.

"You are so big," Gwen said.

Beau looked at Gwen and smiled.

"How old are you?" she said.

Beau held up four fingers. "I'm four," he said proudly.

Leigh tried to be stoic standing there as everyone looked at the crying woman and the cute little boy.

Josh walked up and introduced himself. He introduced his wife, Jen, and their almost five-year-old son, JJ. Leigh's eyes widened as she saw the resemblance between the two young boys.

Gwen spoke to Leigh. "He's very cute."

"Thank you, Gwen," said Leigh. Then she began to cry again. So did Gwen.

Then the most surprising thing of the entire morning happened. Gwen looked back at Jane and then stepped toward Leigh.

"Here," said Gwen. She reached out, put her arms around Leigh, and hugged her. Leigh lost it. She was surprised and grateful all at the same time. Leigh unconsciously sobbed out loud for a second. Beau turned and looked up to see what was going on.

Jane stood up and started to walk over. Then she stopped herself.

No, she thought. *Let's see if this works itself out.*

Leigh didn't cry very long, and Gwen accepted and forgave her. Jane, Josh, and everyone watched the humble scene of true apology, public contrition, and absolution.

Then Gwen asked Leigh to sit down, and the two women talked about Beau and how much he resembled his dad and paternal family.

The rest of the time went very well. It was beautiful "Indian summer" late October day. The group ate the pizza lunch they had ordered in and sat and talked until midafternoon. Everyone took Leigh's navy address card, and Leigh wrote down everyone's addresses and contact information. They agreed to meet again or come to Ohio to visit.

When the day was over, Jane and Gwen followed Leigh to her car as she put Beau into his child seat.

"I'm glad you came," said Gwen. "I really enjoyed getting to see Beau."

"I'm glad I came too," said Leigh. "And I'm so glad all of you could see how much Beau has grown."

Then Gwen turned and said something Jane hadn't expected to hear, at least not yet.

"Leigh, would you come back to the house? Kelly has a ton of stuff that Beau would like to see, that he would be proud for Beau to see."

Leigh looked at Gwen with surprise in her eyes. "Yes," she answered. Leigh noticed that Jane seemed fine with it too.

Ben, Laura, and Kelly's daughter, Jeanne, said their good-byes at the park and drove back to their homes in Galena and Sedalia. The rest of the group caravanned to the farm, including Josh's family.

Beau looked with fascination at the pictures of Kelly. He had seen pictures of him that Leigh kept, but these new ones told much more about his real dad, Kelly. Every now and then Beau asked questions, and Gwen was happy to answer.

Kelly had kept his caps on a deer mount antler rack, and they were still there. Beau looked up with fascination at all the different colored caps. Gwen saw that.

She reached up and pulled several of them down. "Would you like to try some on?" she asked. Gwen put a white sailor hat on him first. He looked cute as could be.

They proceeded to try on Kelly's ag journalism caps and his blue navy ones.

"Would you like to have one of these?"

"Yes," he said as he pointed at the blue navy public affairs cap.

"Then here," said Gwen as she handed him the dark navy-blue cap.

Gwen asked Leigh if she and Beau would like to stay for dinner. "I put a roast in the oven before we went to the park," she said. "There would be plenty for you too!"

They all ate Gwen's big roast with mashed potatoes and gravy, and everyone enjoyed the southern farm family dinner. After supper, Leigh said that she had better get going.

"I need to get some miles behind us before bed tonight," Leigh said.

But Gwen wanted to show Leigh and Beau something else.

"Leigh, Kelly made a fence for our church right before he left for Iraq. Could you and Beau come see that and leave from there to go back home?"

"Well … yes," Leigh said. "Your church isn't far from here, is it?"

"It's less than five miles," Gwen said. "JJ, do you want to go too?" she asked her grandson.

"Yep," he answered. "It would be fun!"

Josh and Jen said their good-byes to Leigh and Beau and stayed at the house. They made sure to invite Beau to come and visit in Kansas City. Leigh did the same with an invitation to Ohio.

Gwen led the way as she and Leigh drove to the Christian church in Sherwin, just west of Columbus. Beau was wearing the blue navy cap Gwen had given him. He laid it on the seat when they arrived.

As they got out of the cars, Gwen spoke to Beau. "Would you like to see the fence your dad, Kelly, made?" she asked.

"Sure," said Beau. "Is it a big one?"

"It's a big white one," said Gwen.

Beau's light blond hair shined brightly in the evening sun as he and JJ bounded over the gravel cross street to the glistening white board railings. Gwen and Leigh watched as the boys climbed to the top board. It was hard to tell which boy was which.

Leigh was amazed at what Kelly had built. But the verse he had written on the railings shocked her with awe: *Greater love hath no man than this, that he lay down his life for his friends," John 15:13, Sherwin Christian Church.*

Leigh looked with her mouth open for several seconds before she spoke.

"Did the man know what would happen?" Leigh said out loud.

Gwen was more used to seeing it than Leigh.

"It really makes you think," she replied, realizing Leigh's disbelief at the verse Kelly had painted before he left for Iraq. It was almost like he had instinctively written it for people to remember.

But Gwen was more enthused at seeing the boys together and watching them experience something that Kelly had built.

"Kelly would be so proud to see his son and grandson today," Gwen said, glowing.

Tears of joy ran down Leigh's cheeks as she saw Beau getting to do exactly what she had wanted for him, what he would want and remember forever.

As the sun began to set, both women looked at the idyllic picture of the boys on the top rail of Kelly's white fence. The women would treasure this memory forever.

Leigh looked at her watch and said they were going to have to go. She motioned for Beau to come back. Gwen did the same for JJ.

"Come on, Beau," said JJ. "Grandma Gwen and your mom are ready to go!"

Gwen and Leigh watched both boys run back to the cars. The backs of their tennis shoes kicked up dust as they crossed the gravel road—two typical blue jean clad boys running where they went at a common midwestern rural church. They reached Gwen's Impala and Leigh's SUV.

Beau grinned big as he climbed in and jumped into his SUV child booster seat. He put his blue navy cap back on. It was Gwen who leaned in to give him a big hug and kiss and then fasten him in. Both she and Leigh began to cry as they hugged it out one last time, before Leigh got into the driver's seat.

"Thank you, Gwen," she said. "This is so good for Beau!"

Gwen wanted to make sure she invited Beau to come back.

"Let's do this again," she said, "and maybe Bill could come too."

"Yes, we will. He will," Leigh answered.

She and Beau waved to new grandma Gwen and JJ.

Leigh sighed with relief as she pulled away from the church. Her heart was as full of joy as it could be.

God answered my deepest prayer today, Leigh said to herself. *My little boy knows his real dad and his family!*

Leigh and Beau turned their SUV east and headed down the Kansas highway, back toward their home in Ohio.

Printed in the United States
By Bookmasters